ENCOUNTER NEAR VENUS

Books by Leonard Wibberley

✡ ✡ ✡

Biography

TIME OF THE HARVEST
Thomas Jefferson, the Years 1801–1826

THE GALES OF SPRING
Thomas Jefferson, the Years 1789–1801

A DAWN IN THE TREES
Thomas Jefferson, the Years 1776 to 1789

YOUNG MAN FROM THE PIEDMONT
The Youth of Thomas Jefferson

THE LIFE OF WINSTON CHURCHILL

WES POWELL, CONQUEROR OF THE GRAND CANYON

JOHN BARRY, FATHER OF THE NAVY

THE WOUND OF PETER WAYNE

KEVIN O'CONNOR AND THE LIGHT BRIGADE

The Treegate Chronicle of the Revolutionary War

JOHN TREEGATE'S MUSKET

PETER TREEGATE'S WAR

SEA CAPTAIN FROM SALEM

TREEGATE'S RAIDERS

ENCOUNTER NEAR V·E·N·U·S

by Leonard Wibberley

Illustrated by Alice Wadowski-Bak

NEW 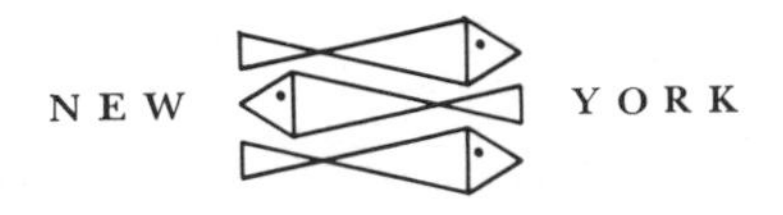 YORK

FARRAR, STRAUS AND GIROUX

An Ariel Book

Library of Congress catalog card number: AC 67–10376

FIRST PRINTING, 1967

Ariel Books, a division of
Farrar, Straus and Giroux
Published simultaneously in Canada by
Ambassador Books, Ltd., Rexdale, Ontario
Printed in the United States of America
by American Book–Stratford Press, Inc., New York

DESIGNED BY HERB JOHNSON

DEDICATION

I am not fond of children, but having been asked for a dedication for this account of my journey to Nede, I offer it to the four children who were thrust upon me by their parents and became my companions on the voyage—Kevin, Patricia, Christopher, and the smaller one whose name was, I think, Arabella. For children, they were quite tolerable companions.

The Impatient Wise One

P.S. Their father is a complete nincompoop.

ENCOUNTER NEAR VENUS

CHAPTER ONE

A GIRL who, if she were not wearing jeans, might have been a princess was sitting on the floor brushing her long hair, which was the color of honey with burned toast mixed into it. She made smooth, patient, soothing strokes with her brush until she got to the ends, when the brush usually stuck, and she said, "Bother," and tugged at it and then started another smooth patient soothing stroke. Her mouth was slightly open while she did this, and she had a dreamy look, for she was thinking of a variety of things and none of them had much connection with each other.

She was thinking of Herman and his Hermits and graduating from junior high school (for which event she had made a beautiful pale blue dress of real silk) and whether she would be allowed to go to a school dance, which she hadn't dared to mention to her mother and father yet, and behind all these somewhat pleasant thoughts she thought of Coppertown and that wasn't pleasant at all.

Coppertown was in Colorado and was where she was to spend eight weeks of her summer vacation. She would prefer to stay at the beach in California, where there would be ample opportunity to wear her new swimsuit, which had a ruffled top and (for use when not swimming) a straw boater, and the whole ensemble was both "boss" and "camp." Such an outfit could scarcely be worn with any aplomb in Coppertown.

The girl's name was Patricia.

She didn't like Coppertown. She didn't like the name to start with. It had no style, no swing, no grace. It was as ugly as a pot. For a town which mined copper to call itself Coppertown was so flatfooted as to suggest that it was inhabited entirely by plain, ugly, unimaginative people who had never heard of Herman and his Hermits and certainly knew nothing of 1914-style swimsuits. So she brushed her hair, looking into a television set instead of a graceful oval mirror, and thought with vague dismay of Coppertown.

Patricia was not alone in the room. With her was her small sister, Arabella, just ten. She didn't want to go to Coppertown either, and she even refused to say the name. She called it "that place," with an air of oppressed innocence. There was in Arabella an enchanting mixture of saint and sorceress. She did not want to go to Coppertown because she couldn't take her kittens with her. There were five of them. One of them was black and white, one of them was dove gray and white. Three of them were a wild mixture of ginger and black and white, all in patches. They were patchwork kittens in the same way that quilts used to be patchwork quilts. One of the patchwork kittens had a black mustache and was called Pancho. They were all as fat as butter tubs and had fat pointy tails, and they only purred when they were feeding, which was whenever they could corner their mother.

But Arabella had been told that she could not take the kittens to "that place"—the horrible place in Colorado where it was plain that there wasn't a kitten or any kind of animal but only a lot of grim, lean, unsmiling people dressed in dirty clothes from mining copper, which they did day and night.

"It's like being sent to prison," said Arabella to herself, and she pulled Pancho out of the milk bowl, for Pancho had not yet discovered that milk was not for wading in. She wiped one end of Pancho while Pancho's mother tackled the other end with a few vigorous swipes of her tongue, and between the two of them they got the milk off the kitten.

With the two girls were two boys, their brothers, and they didn't want to go to Coppertown either. The oldest was engaged in a feat of astonishing mental agility, for he was reading Hawthorne's *The Scarlet Letter* while watching a Western on television. One part of his brain was saying, or recording, "From the intense consciousness of being the object of severe and universal observation, the wearer of the scarlet letter was at length relieved, by discerning, on the outskirts of the crowd, a figure which irresistibly took possession of her thoughts." Another part of his brain watched a man crouched behind a rock in Western mountain territory shooting at another man similarly located some distance away. The gun exploded like French .75's and the bullets went "whing . . . zing . . . pock . . . powie" against the rocks.

Hester Prynne in the book gave her baby a convulsive squeeze, and it "uttered another cry of pain." On the television set one of the men was shot and a dark stain appeared on his shirt front and he grunted. Then a blond girl drove across the screen in a beautiful car, and the boy's brain cleverly identified this as having nothing to do with Nathaniel Hawthorne or the Western gunfight, being only the commercial, and immediately rejected it.

This boy's name was Kevin, he was sixteen, and his mind was busy with other things as well. He thought of a wave as lovely as green glass, its sides glittering and quick with joyous movement. He thought of himself sitting on his surfboard watching this perfect wave approaching. He thought of driving his arms into the water and paddling so the board could pick up speed. He thought of the quickening of the board beneath him as the wave caught it and of himself standing up and lancing toward the beach on this rolling emerald of a wave in the sun and the light and the water, the world all speed and laughter and joy. Then he turned to the Reverend Mr. Dimmesdale, and that put him immediately in mind of Coppertown and he said, right in the middle of the ordeal of Hester Prynne, "Nuts."

There would be no surf at Coppertown, Colorado that was sure. For eight weeks of a magnificent summer he would be separated from the surf and his surfboard. In addition he had to do a book report on *The Scarlet Letter*. Nothing could be more frustrating.

His brother, Christopher, was lying in bed also watching the Western, for the TV set was in his bedroom. He was lying in bed because he wanted to be a professional ballplayer and he had read that rest was important. So whenever he wasn't playing ball or eating, he rested. When he first heard that all four of them were to spend eight weeks of the summer with their uncle at Coppertown, he had been delighted because he thought they were going to Cooperstown, where the Baseball Hall of Fame was located. When that error was corrected, he squinted up his eyes and cocked his head to one side (these being gestures of his when thinking) and asked with the cunning of a Machiavelli, "What about Pony League?"

"What *about* Pony League?" demanded his father, throwing the question back at his son as if he had been presented with some kind of completely unworthy offering.

"Well, I'm supposed to pitch for the Cardinals. Me and Grimey."

"Well, it will be Grimey and someone else pitching

for the Cardinals," said his father, "because you are going to your uncle's at Coppertown."

"Gee," said Christopher. Then he brightened. "Couldn't I stay with the Fredricks?"

"No," said his father. "They are friends of ours. Eight weeks of you and they would be suing us. The man is a lawyer." And so the four children sat in the room, one brushing her hair, one playing with kittens, one resting to be a ballplayer, and the other glooming over the girl with the capital A beautifully embroidered on the front of her dress.

Ahead of all these children lay eight weeks of Coppertown. And for that there was no consolation.

CHAPTER TWO

A PLANE took the children to Coppertown. The plane, after the excitement of taking off, and the mixed feeling of relief and disappointment that it had not crashed in the process, was a bore. There was nothing to do except read magazines or look out the window at acres and acres of cottony clouds far, far below, each one different and yet all looking the same. It was hard to believe that such infinite variety could produce such appalling monotony.

Now and again in a gap in the clouds a piece of shadowed land appeared, so distant that it seemed to belong to another time and indeed another and unreachable planet, something perhaps out of a fairy tale or a work of science fiction. Patricia amused herself with this fancy for a while. She thought vaguely of the world as a place that had been put under an enchantment. Nobody had been allowed to land on it for a thousand years, and those in the plane were the first to try to break the spell. They were circling, hidden from the evil watchers below by the canopy of cloud, looking through their radar for a place where they could land without being discovered.

While she thought of this, Arabella, who was sitting nearest the window because she was the youngest, said, "Look. A flying saucer. A pink one."

Patricia looked and saw it right away. It wasn't much like a saucer, but like two pudding bowls, one on top of the other, and with a spinning disk of some kind around the middle. "Kevin," she cried. "Look!" And she pounced on her brother, who was in the front seat, and he looked too and saw just a little fragment of the shining disk and then it was gone. Christopher didn't see anything because he was resting up to be a ballplayer.

The stewardess, seeing the excitement, came up. "Anything the matter?" she asked.

"I just saw a flying saucer," said Patricia.

"A pink one," said Arabella.

The stewardess bent down a little and looked out the window, more or less for politeness, and shrugged. "Would you like something to drink?" she asked.

"It was like two mixing bowls with a fringe around them," said Patricia.

The stewardess smiled. "Coke?" she said.

"Yes, thank you," said Patricia.

"A pink one," said Arabella.

"I think it was the sun through the portholes," said

the stewardess. "We are flying northeast and the sun is to the west of us and makes an angle on the glass."

When the stewardess had gone, Patricia leaned over to Kevin and said, "I really did see it, though. Honest. It looked like it was real near, but it might have been a hundred miles away."

"Maybe it was just the sun," said Kevin. "What I saw could have been the sun."

"Who would believe that the sun could make two big pink mixing bowls with a thing like a ballet skirt around them?" asked Patricia with scorn.

They took the Cokes and watched again, but they didn't see anything. The people nearby in the plane were divided in their opinions about what Patricia and Arabella had seen. Some thought they were joking. Some thought they were trying to draw attention to themselves. Some questioned them sharply, almost angrily, about the flying saucer and tried to make Patricia's description conform with their own mental picture of a flying saucer.

One man, who lived at what he called Four Corners, said several flying saucers had landed near his home and he had spoken to the people in them. He had taken pictures, but they didn't come out very well. He said he'd been for a ride in one. He started to tell everybody about it, and then people got a sort of stony look on their faces and his voice trailed off and he stopped talking and picked up a magazine. Patricia felt sorry for him.

Although they watched like hawks, none of them saw a flying saucer again, and eventually, between the muted vibrations of the plane and the hypnotism of the slowly moving cloudscape, Patricia, Arabella, and Kevin fell asleep. When these three were asleep, Christopher woke up. He woke up by his usual method—rocking his head vigorously from side to side, then wriggling his nose, and then moving his shoulders around in a kind of a shimmy. It was, perhaps, his method of checking that there had been an improvement rather than a deterioration of his conditioning while he was asleep, bearing in mind that sleep was a method of training for professional ball.

When he had done all these things, he opened his eyes and allowed the world to slip slowly into his consciousness. He adjusted to the fact that he was in an airplane, that the ceiling was covered with stuff with little holes in it, that his brother and sisters were asleep, and (from the empty container) that Kevin had had a Coke, which he had not, and that was unfair.

Distressed at this treachery, he turned his eyes from his brother to look out the window. The sun, far to the west now, touched the clouds with gold tinged with pink. The faces of the clouds away from the sun were dark, cold, mysterious, and of enormous depth. Here and there pinnacles of cloud, gleaming on one side and deep purple on the other, soared out of the field of clouds and threw a shadow across the cloud land—a shadow perhaps as much as a hundred miles long and full of mystery.

Christopher looked at this landscape of cloud thoughtfully and saw a tiny round spot appear from the shadow behind one glittering tower. It looked like a baseball. In fact, he was about to poke Kevin in the ribs and say, "Hey, look at that little cloud that looks like a baseball," when he realized that the cloud was zooming toward the plane. It came at tremendous speed, increasing in size, and then quite suddenly it was a huge thing, pink with a shining disk around it which flashed under the plane and was gone.

"What do you know!" cried Christopher. "An outside curve and a slider combined."

He looked around for someone else who had seen this astonishing happening. Across the aisle, a hard-faced little man in an overcoat which was much too big for him was looking out of the window, half standing and straining to see.

"Did you see it?" asked Christopher.

The man looked at him. "See what?" he demanded quite fiercely.

"That thing that went by in a slider and a curve."

"You mean the flying saucer?" asked the man.

"Yes," said Christopher.

"Nope," said the man, his face quite without expression. "I didn't see it." He paused and then demanded, "You want a Coke?"

"Yes," said Christopher, though he didn't see what that had got to do with it.

"Well, tell the stewardess that you just saw a flying saucer," said the man.

Christopher called the stewardess and told her he had seen a flying saucer. She smiled and bent down and looked out the window and said it was the angle of the sun on the glass and explained how the plane was going northeast and the sun was in the west and that was what did it. Then she asked Christopher whether he would like a Coke and he said yes, and she brought one. Then the little man across the aisle, talking from behind the back of his hand in a hoarse whisper, said, "Get what I mean? It's a conspiracy of silence. They're trying to keep it a secret."

Christopher leaned back in his seat to drink his Coke and think about this.

CHAPTER THREE

AFTER a while it seemed to Christopher, who was the more thoughtful and least talkative of the four children, that the plane was beginning to lose altitude. Either that or the pinnacles of cloud, shining on their western sides and dark with purple shadow on the opposite, were rising higher, for the plane, which had first been over the tops of these pinnacles, now flew level with them, and a little later below the tops, so that it was flying through a series of stately columns that were at first far apart and then began to be more closely spaced.

The boy got the impression after a while that they were flying past the pillars of one of those ruined Greek temples he had seen pictures of in his history books. But this temple was colossal, the distance from pillar to pillar being half a mile and the pillars themselves twenty miles high or even higher. They threw across the gleaming floor of cloud (or could it be marble?) a shadow that reached to the horizon, and over their glowing tops was a roof alive with blue light, which was, of course, the sky, or could it be lapis lazuli?

When the plane passed on the eastern side of one of the pinnacles, it entered a shadow as dense and cold as that made by a pillar of stone, and the boy noted that the pilot never flew the plane through any of these pillars, which he would surely have done if they were cloud, but altered course to miss them, and by a good margin. It was all very odd, and Christopher was tempted to wake up Kevin, for it seemed to him that something extraordinary was going to happen to them soon. But he decided against this, lest Kevin by some remark should shatter the wonderful illusion into which he felt himself penetrating.

He knew now that the plane was coming down. He could feel it losing height as it sped between the golden pillars to the white floor below. As the plane approached this floor, rather like a fly in a temple about to land on the marble paving, Christopher braced himself. He expected a shock, either the shock of landing or the shock of a terrible impact as the plane crashed onto the floor.

He did not brace himself by leaning back in his seat, for he was looking out the window. But he stiffened himself against the wall of the plane and the arm of his seat, awaiting the crash. He had time to note the steady draining of the light as they descended and saw a bloom of moisture collect on the wing of the plane, turning it from bright silver to dull gray. Then they passed into a deep shadow behind one of the cloud pillars and plunged down quite swiftly into this shadow. Christopher shut his eyes tight, his nerves straining, and waited for a crash.

Nothing happened. The shadow increased to utter darkness. Christopher opened his eyes, feeling the plane still dropping, and saw a little yellow light below and ahead of them. They passed over it, and then the plane leveled and the tires started to squeal and grunt and bump as the plane was landed on what seemed to be an inadequate runway.

"Coppertown," said the stewardess, coming up to the children. "Hurry. We can only spend a minute here. We are behind schedule. Why didn't you fasten your safety belts when the light went on?"

"They were asleep," said Christopher.

"That won't do," said the stewardess. "You must fasten them. It's in the rules. Now, do hurry. The pilot says we must be leaving right away."

She seemed in a desperate hurry to get them out of the plane, as if something disastrous would happen if the plane remained long on the ground. She grabbed their hand luggage from the rack overhead and hustled to the door with it, and the children took the rest and came along, Arabella and Tricia quite awake but Kevin still sleepy and confused, for he had been hurled from the back of a hissing sapphire wave to the interior of an airplane, which is enough to confuse anybody. Riding the wave with him, on an old-fashioned fifteen-foot board, had been a Hawaiian boy of his own age, wearing a necklace of white and red coral.

"I didn't get his name," he said to Christopher.

"What?" asked Christopher.

"Forget it," said Kevin. He was conscious now that they had to get off and turned around and said to the stewardess, "Isn't anybody else getting off here?"

"No. It isn't a scheduled stop. We are obliged to land here on request to keep our franchise, and you are the passengers for whom a landing was requested. Please do hurry." She had the door open and the steps lowered down the plane to the ground. The light from the plane illuminated the top of the steps, but the bottom was in shadow.

Tricia and Arabella hesitated at the top, and Christopher, who was also standing there, looked about for the huge temple pillars he had seen, but could find nothing and felt sad.

Kevin said, "Okay. Let's get out of here, you kids," and started down the gangway holding his bag and an overcoat. The others, a little hesitantly, went down the steps, and when they were at the bottom the stewardess said, "I hope you had a pleasant flight. Good luck," and the steps were retracted and the door of the plane closed.

The four children looked around. There was enough light for them to see each other in outline but not in detail. They could see no path from the runway to an airport building of any kind. They stood in darkness, uncertain of where to go, huddled together, their hearts beating a little faster than usual.

"We'd better get off the runway," said Kevin. "Come on." He walked away from the plane, the others following, and it was just as well that they did, for no sooner were they clear of it than the engine whined into life and the plane trundled off and lanced into the sky, leaving utter solitude behind.

"I wonder what she meant by 'Good luck,' " said Christopher, who had been thinking of this remark of the stewardess's.

"I don't like it here," said Arabella.

"It's spooky," said Patricia.

"What a heck of a way to run an airline," said Kevin. "Dump you out in the middle of nowhere and take off. Well, come on."

It was all very well to say "come on," but the problem was "Come on, where to?" because there still was not a light to be seen, nor the outline of a building nor anything at all but the dark around. But Kevin, having said "Come on," started off to his right, for no other reason than that he had to move somewhere, and the others followed in silence.

For the first fifty yards they walked on a hard surface which might have been concrete or tarmac and was undoubtedly part of the runway. Then they came to grass, which was thick and tangled and wet. There they stopped. There was a little more light now, or perhaps it was that their eyes were accustomed to the dark and they could see better. Rather than set off across the thick grass, they moved along the edge of it and were rewarded by finding a small pathway leading away from the runway. They took this and found that it led up a hill no more than a hundred feet high and with a slight slope.

"This hill is the reason we couldn't see anything from the runway," said Kevin. "The runway is sort of in the bottom of a bowl. When we get to the top of the hill, we will find some kind of building."

"I hope so," said Arabella. "I'm hungry."

Christopher, as usual, had been thinking while walking. "How did you know to set out in this direction?" he asked.

"I don't know. It felt right, that's all," said Kevin.

"That's funny," said Christopher. "It feels right to me as if somebody told me it was right. Back there on the runway."

"Instinct," said Kevin, but this reply didn't satisfy Christopher. As they plodded up the hill, it seemed to him that he could see, off to the side of them, little flashes of light appearing and disappearing. There were not many—just two or three—and he always saw them out of the tail of his eye. When he turned directly to look where they had appeared, he saw nothing. He decided not to say anything about this, but he had a vague impression that they were being herded in the direction in which they were going.

When they were on the runway, the sky had been

covered with tremendously dense clouds. These now moved off. Stars were twinkling overhead, and the landscape around was frosted with starlight. The starlight revealed that the pathway led through a forest of tremendous trees. The trees ended a hundred feet or more on either side of the pathway, but they rose as tall as skyscrapers against the night sky, and the little lights that Christopher saw or thought he saw came from within this impressive forest. To judge by the shape of their tops against the sky, the trees were firs or pines. Now and again a slight wind rustled their tops, producing a little sighing moan, which made Tricia move a little nearer to Arabella.

"Pancakes," said Arabella, still thinking how hungry she was, "with a lot of strawberry jam on them."

"There's a house ahead," said Kevin, who, being in the lead, had reached the top of the hill first. "I hope it's Uncle Bill's house. It looks kind of odd."

CHAPTER FOUR

In the pale light of the stars, they could see that the house lay in an enormous square clearing surrounded by the dark wall of the forest trees. The clearing was covered with grass which had a silvery look in the starlight, and the grass was close-clipped, like a beautifully tailored lawn. A lawn it was, but a lawn of perhaps twenty acres in extent, with not a flower bed or shrub to break its monotony. The only interruption of this level expanse was the house, which was an odd house indeed.

It was odd in that it was old-fashioned, for it was at least three stories high and the roof was a jumble of gables and chimneys, and erupting from these were perhaps half a dozen masts or antennas, some with a series of rods laid horizontally across their tops and others with a kind of latticework of wire. These could be clearly seen, for they interrupted the luminous sky with dark lines.

"Color TV," said Arabella, who was not impressed by

architecture. But the hugeness of this house made Patricia uneasy. It was a grotesque place, and the conclusion was inescapable that it was inhabited by a grotesque person.

"I wonder what sort of a person Uncle Bill really is," she said, and reflected that they really knew very little about him except that he was unmarried and lived in Coppertown.

"We'll soon find out," said Kevin. "You'd have thought he would have been down at the runway to meet us."

"I hope he knew we were coming," said Patricia.

"Sure he did," said Kevin. "Dad sent him a telegram giving the plane and flight and time of arrival and all that stuff."

"Maybe he didn't get it," said Christopher thoughtfully.

"He better had," said Arabella. "I'm hungry."

There was a light in one of the rooms on the ground floor of the house, but not a very bright one, for it illuminated only the area about it rather than the whole room. The pathway led down the hill to the tremendous level lawn, in the center of which the house was situated. As they hurried along the pathway, it seemed to Christopher that the dots of light he kept seeing had left the trees and were moving along beside them over the lawn. He kept seeing the flashes, but never directly, and Kevin saw them too, for he said they were fireflies.

When they were perhaps a hundred feet from the house, the solitary light in the downstairs room went out. It didn't go out quickly like a light bulb turned off, but diminished slowly in brilliance to the smallest perceptible glow and then was gone.

None of the children liked that, and they would at this point have turned back and gone somewhere else, had there been somewhere else to go. The house, now completely dark, loomed high above them into the sky with its mad collection of gables and antennas. The children stopped and stared at the house, uncertain whether they should knock or flee, and saw the flickering lights around out of the corners of their eyes. Then Christopher saw a small whitish thing lying before the gloomy front door. He picked it up and found that it was a Western Union telegram, and although there was not enough light to read the address, they guessed that it was meant for their uncle and probably was the telegram their father had sent telling him of the time of their arrival.

The telegram was a great comfort to them. The fact that this gargoyle of a house was visited by workaday people like Western Union messengers deprived it of much of its menace. So Kevin went to the front door to knock or ring a bell if he could find one, and as soon as he got there the door swung open, and without a sound.

In the gaping darkness of what seemed to be a corridor there was a glow of light, soft and slightly blue so as to be gentle on the eyes. It approached very slowly and then moved back down the corridor, stopped, approached again, and again moved away, as if inviting and even pleading with them to come in.

The light was no trick played on the eyes, for they all saw it, and they were all petrified. All together they turned to run, only to find that outside the doorway there was now a ring of these lights, advancing toward them and then retreating, as if trying to push them or coax them into the house.

The lights certainly were not fireflies, and they seemed possessed of intelligence and, in fact, good will. Certainly the first panic at seeing them was soon gone, and Patricia said, "I don't know what they are, but I don't think they'll hurt us."

"If they were going to hurt us," said Christopher, "they could have done it by now."

"I get the feeling that they're trying to tell us to go into the house," said Kevin.

"Me too," said Christopher.

Arabella, who was very fond of pets and had never had a pet light before, grew bold enough to hold out her hand. One of the lights approached like Tinker Bell and allowed a little drop of itself to fall into her palm, where it glowed beautifully, without causing her the slightest pain. "It feels lovely," she said. "Like warm fur and ice at the same time."

"I don't understand it," said Kevin, "but let's go on in."

They went inside, the lights flowing after them, and they were ushered by the lights into a large sitting room that gave off from the right-hand side of the corridor. The sitting room had plenty of chairs and couches in it, but all belonging to the time of President Taft.

The furniture was of heavy mahogany, carved in curlicues of flowers and tendrils, and the legs of the chairs ended in animal or bird claws. There was a monstrous grand piano in the room, covered with a shawl big enough to have been a carpet. There was a stool before the piano, the legs terminating on the floor in claws, each grasping a small crystal ball not much bigger than a glass marble.

The children could see all these things because of the friendly lights, which seemed to anticipate their desires and moved to any object they wanted to look at so as to illuminate it. In this manner the lights moved from the piano to the chairs to the couches, to the carpets, to brass bowls containing plants, and then to the walls to show the old flowered wallpaper, and finally, all cooperating, grouped themselves around a huge oil painting that hung on the wall.

The subject of the painting was so out of place in this antiquated room that the children were shocked. It showed a man in a space suit such as the astronauts use, standing upright, with his arms outstretched, and in each hand a number of the friendly bluish lights. And in the background, quite distinct, so that it could not possible be taken for anything else, was a flying saucer. A pink one.

The children knew immediately that the man was their Uncle Bill.

CHAPTER FIVE

It was Kevin who first suspected that the lights, who it was now plain were some kind of being or personality and not merely a cool flame, might be able to communicate in some way other than moving about. They certainly seemed to know what was in his mind and the minds of his sisters and his brother, so there was no problem really of communicating with them. Rather it was the other way around, the lights communicating with him and the others.

Examining the painting of the man who must be his uncle, with the lights on his hands, just as Arabella had taken the tiny drop of light in her palm (it was now on her head and looked very fetching), Kevin decided that his uncle had met these creatures on some other planet, brought them to earth, and must surely have found a way of talking with them.

"Be quiet, you kids," he said, for having recovered from their shock, they were all gabbling about the picture. "I want to see if I can talk to these lights." The children stopped talking immediately, and the lights, which had grouped themselves along the frame of the picture like the electric light bulbs that are put around the makeup mirrors of actors and actresses, seemed themselves to be straining with expectancy.

"You lights," said Kevin. "Can you talk?"

The effect was astonishing. There wasn't the slightest whisper of a reply, but instead the lights started flashing on and off, hopping up and down, bumping into each other and generally behaving as if either in a panic or carried away with an excess of joy.

"What do you know?" said Kevin. "They're trying to say something." At this the lights redoubled their efforts, flashing and blipping and glowing and dimming and making themselves long and short and bright and dull all over the picture frame, and the effect, though visual, was that of a crowd of people all trying to say something different at the same time.

Eventually one of them traveled all along the frame, colliding with the others as if bopping them on the head, and he whirled around the picture frame a couple of times in an apparent effort to restore some order. All the other lights got the message and stopped signaling, contenting themselves with glowing in a quiet but expectant manner.

Satisfied that matters were now under control, the light who had taken over command perched itself on the top of the picture frame in the center and with great deliberation, as if making a public address that had been

painfully and carefully rehearsed many times, did a little blip and then a longer blip. The children watched this performance without understanding the message. The light did the same thing again. Christopher screwed up his eyes and cocked his head on one side.

"I don't get it," said Kevin.

"I do," said Christopher. "It's Morse. What other way would a light talk?"

But they didn't know any Morse, that being one of the many things that both Kevin and Christopher had decided they would learn when they got around to it. But they had not gotten around to it.

The lights, who seemed to know everything that was passing in the children's minds, were very surprised that they did not know the Morse code. They seemed to expect that all humans knew how to communicate in Morse, and they started gabbling among themselves about it, or rather all blinking on and off and hopping to one side and then the other and up and down until the central light restored order by tearing around the picture frame and bumping them all.

Then he twinkled in the manner of a star, only faster, and half a dozen of the lights left the picture frame and floated across the room to a bookshelf that ran along one wall. Here, after a little searching, they clustered around one thick volume. Kevin went to it and read on the spine the words *International Signal Codes.* He took the volume down, the lights bobbing up and down in excitement and approval, and looked in the index.

Morse code was among the headings listed, and he turned to the pages indicated. This produced almost a cheer from the lights, which all hopped up a little in the air together and down again and did this three times.

Then the lights that had guided Kevin to the volume formed a circle around his head like a halo—a charming reward for using just a little intelligence.

With the signal book open before him at the pages containing the symbols of the Morse code, Kevin and the others turned to watch the light (though no brighter than the others, it seemed to be the chief light) that was trying to signal them. But all was not plain sailing even then. They had trouble distinguishing dots from dashes and remembering how many dots and how many dashes had been transmitted in a series and in what order. It was the work of half an hour to get five letters, and whenever they got one, the lights, not at all impatient but rather enormously good-natured and encouraging, made a halo around the head of whichever of the children announced the letter.

When they got the five letters, however, and the signals were stopped and all the lights waited expectantly, they found that the letters did not form a word. They were N H Y L C. The children stared at this blankly, watched by the expectant lights, including the tiny light that had become Arabella's pet and had left her head and was now glowing on her wrist like a lovely jewel.

"Do you suppose it's his name?" asked Christopher,

and it seemed that the lights, disappointed, grew a little dimmer.

"Of course not," said Patricia. "If you want to say something to a stranger, you don't just go up and say 'Joe' to them, or 'Bob,' or something. You tell them something."

"Okay," said Kevin. "It's a message. It doesn't spell anything, so the message is in code."

"Hey, how about some kind of signal code?" cried Christopher, excited. "I don't mean just Morse code, I mean a code using Morse code. Like if a ship were sinking, the captain wouldn't put up a lot of flags spelling out 'I'm sinking.' There must be just one flag or one letter that means that."

Christopher was rewarded for this piece of deduction by a positive crown of lights that whirled around his head like a blazing merry-go-round. Kevin had already turned to the end of the signal book and found an international code that gave a special significance to each letter transmitted in Morse by lights, by sound, or by flags.

"Here it is," he cried, and this is what came out of the jumble of letters.

N No

H Pilot on Board

Y Carrying Mails

L Something to Communicate

C Yes

"It makes some kind of sense," said Patricia, trying to see to the top of her head, because she hadn't won a circle of lights yet. " 'No pilot on board' would mean that Uncle Bill isn't here, though we know that already. And 'carrying mails,' 'something to communicate' means he left a message for us." But she got no halo for this.

"That's obvious," said Kevin a little sarcastically. "But what does 'Yes' mean on the end of it?"

"That letter didn't come until a little while after the first four, and when we got them I was wondering whether it was a code and then came the letter meaning 'Yes.' So it was answering me and not part of the message," said Patricia. She was immediately rewarded with a wonderful corona of double lights, and blushed with pleasure.

"Where's the message?" asked Kevin, expecting that the lights would stream off and show him a desk drawer. But instead they gathered again around the picture frame (it seemed a favorite spot of theirs, and afterward the children learned that when their uncle was away the lights gathered around the picture because they were fond of him and felt lonely). Once again, the chief light started to signal. Strangely, although they all looked alike, being a soft flame like that produced by an oil lamp, only of a pale blue tinge instead of butter yellow, they began to impress the children, each one of them with a personality of its own. The children were, for instance, able to pick out the chief light from the others, though it was the same size and color, and also the light that had given a tiny piece of itself to Arabella. But how they were able to do this, they were not at all sure.

The light started signaling again, but this time in plain Morse, and the first word was YOUR, which was followed by UNCLE and then the letters WE. The message got no further than that. The lights suddenly streamed out of the room, going right through the wall to the outside of the house, and the four children, running to the window, could see them like the tail of a bluing comet darting up into the sky. Even the tiny light on Arabella's wrist went with them, though it got a late start and had a hard time catching up, and the children were left in darkness, though not for long.

The sky above the vast lawn area around the house, after a short while, began to get lighter, the light at first being silvery and then turning pink as if dawn were coming. This brightening of the sky threw the dark wall of trees into sharp and bold relief and made them seem all the more foreboding. Brighter and brighter the sky grew, the center of the brightness being over the trees on the right-hand side of the house. Then, like a tremendous sun, a round pinkish shape, hidden from sight for a while by the top of the window through which they were staring, zoomed into view over the trees and settled, as gently as a soap bubble, in front of the house.

As soon as it was on the ground, two things happened to it. First the shining disk that formed a flashing equator around the flying saucer disappeared. And then the saucer itself changed color from shell pink to deep pink to red to reddish brown and finally became invisible. At last a hatch opened in the lower half of the saucer and a man descended from it and strode toward the house.

CHAPTER SIX

"YOUR father is an idiot," said Uncle Bill. "Believe me, I know what I'm talking about. I've been his brother for forty years and have yet to discover the slightest trace of anything that could be mistaken for intelligence in his make-up. He sits there writing those books of his, never answering any correspondence, and presumes that whatever he wants to do is perfectly agreeable to everybody else. Sending you here when I went to a great deal of trouble to write to him saying not to do so because I had . . . er, urgent business to attend to."

"When did you write to him?" asked Kevin.

"In plenty of time," said Uncle Bill. "Plenty of time. Yesterday at least."

"But he couldn't possibly have got the letter if it was only mailed yesterday."

"And why not?" demanded Uncle Bill. "Why not, I say? If the world is able to turn completely on its axis in twenty-four hours, and in the process travel several hundreds of thousands of miles through space in its orbit around the sun, why is it impossible for our fiddling post-office department to send a letter in the same period from Colorado to California?"

To this, none of the children attempted an answer, concluding privately that Uncle Bill, being a space traveler, was a bit muddled about time and distance as they applied to earth. But Patricia said, "There's a Western Union telegram for you. I think it is from Daddy telling you the time of the plane we were arriving on." They had brought the telegram into the house and gave it to him. He tore it open, glanced at it by the light of a huge oil lamp that he had lit in the hallway, and snorted.

"That's it," he said. "Absolute idiot, that brother of mine. Buried in books. Completely out of touch with the world. How did he ever expect a telegram to get to me in ten hours from California to Colorado when my letter didn't arrive in twenty-four hours?"

This question was so outrageous that no answer was possible, and Uncle Bill, satisfied that he had made his point, turned to examine the children in some detail, one by one, rather as if he had never seen a child before. They, in turn, examined him, and saw a man rather smaller than the one in the painting, with a large fierce beard, blackish and reddish and touched with white, a head that was bald on the top and had a bump in the bald part but was well covered with hair on the sides, and very blue and fierce eyes.

His nose had a beakish look to it, and really the only

redeeming feature about his face was that there were big wrinkles at the corner of his eyes, indicating that he laughed quite a lot, though he certainly wasn't laughing now.

After having examined each of the children, holding the large oil lamp quite close to them for this purpose, Uncle Bill put the lamp back on the piano and said, "Well, we shall have to send you back in a day or two. Whenever I can arrange for the plane to stop here. That means a message to West Coast Airlines in Denver. I can't keep you here. I have too many things to do. Far too many things to do."

A thought seemed to occur to him, for he said brusquely, "How did you find the house?"

"We just walked in what we thought was the right direction," said Kevin.

"Quite so, quite so, and very intelligent of you too," said Uncle Bill. "Nobody to meet you, of course." The latter was said more in the form of a question than a statement, as if he were trying to discover, without the children's suspecting it, whether they had been met.

"Only the little lights," said Christopher.

"What little lights?" demanded Uncle Bill. "Oh, the fireflies," and he made an attempt at a laugh, which was a kind of a shout and contained no mirth or conviction at all. Then, as if he didn't want any more talk on that subject, he said, "I suppose you are all hungry?"

"Practically starving," said Arabella.

"Well, let's see if we can find something to eat then,"

said Uncle Bill, picking up the oil lamp and leading them out of the room to the kitchen. "I haven't much to offer. What would you like?"

"Pancakes with strawberry jam," said Arabella.

"I always did hate children," said Uncle Bill. "There isn't a pancake in the house. In fact, I haven't seen one since I was a boy, except those Mexican things and I abominate them—to me they taste like the leather tongues from discarded football boots."

They had by now reached the kitchen, a huge, low-ceilinged place with white painted cupboards all around the walls and a tremendous iron stove, polished black, on one side of the room. The top of this stove was quite flat, but there were a lot of circular lids let into it, and Uncle Bill took up a curious implement like a small lever, removed one of these lids, peered down into the stove, grunted, and, going to a box, got newspaper and some small sticks. He screwed the newspaper up into balls and put them in the stove and put sticks on top of it, and then took a piece of candle off the shelf that ran over the stove. This he cut up with a large clasp knife, dropping the pieces of candle into the stove, and then struck a match, and soon he had a fire going very briskly indeed.

"Can I set out some plates?" asked Patricia.

"Yes," said Uncle Bill. "Over in that cupboard there. The blue ones. I'll get the food myself."

He got down on his hands and knees to open one of the low cupboards and started to pull out jar after jar of food, none of which met with his approval. "Can't find a blessed thing," he grumbled. "There were some beans here somewhere."

"Oh no, not beans," said Arabella. "Surely you must have something else besides beans."

"What's your name, little girl?" asked Uncle Bill, turning on her.

"Arabella."

"Hum. You're the one that wanted pancakes."

"Yes, but if you haven't got pancakes and you've only got beans, I'll take cat food."

"What's in all those jars?" asked Patricia from the table.

"Nothing for you. Not food at all, really. Sort of—er . . . stuff."

"Do you have flour—and eggs?"

"I know there are eggs and there's some flour somewhere."

"You must have milk," said Patricia. "Everybody has milk."

They found flour and eggs and milk, and Patricia started to mix pancakes while Uncle Bill looked for some oil to cook them with and grumbled that he hated pancakes and his whole house was being turned upside down. But, despite all his brusqueness and irritation, he didn't really frighten the children, and they waited for him to explain about the lights and the flying saucer in which he had arrived and the picture of himself in the front room in the space suit.

The lights, which had streamed from the house before his arrival, had not returned, and Uncle Bill made quite pathetic attempts, to start with, at pretending that they didn't exist and neither did the flying saucer. But he was very easily cornered. Arabella said she wanted her little light back, and Uncle Bill, instead of pretending that he had not heard her, asked, what little light? Soon Uncle Bill realized that the children knew all about the lights and couldn't be bamboozled into believing that they were fireflies that had been studying Morse code, so he gave up.

"All right," he said. "I've done my best. This situation has been forced on me, and I cannot find any way out of it. I will tell you all about the lights, and everything else. But after dinner. Are you sure you know how to cook pancakes, girl?"

"Yes," said Patricia.

"Well, I don't like pancakes," said Uncle Bill. "I haven't eaten any since I was a boy, and the decision I made then was a very sensible one indeed." But he ate ten of them, and since they hadn't any strawberry jam, they had some of the strange stuff out of the glass jars, which tasted infinitely better.

When they were all full and the dishes were cleared away and washed up, they settled down by the fire, Kevin and Patricia in chairs and Christopher and Arabella on the floor, the firelight playing on their faces and making them look both thoughtful and interested, and Uncle Bill commenced his story.

CHAPTER SEVEN

"You have to pay the closest attention," said Uncle Bill, "but you may ask any questions you wish, because it will all be puzzling to you, and I will answer them.

"I am going to start off with the Diet of Worms because it provides a clue to the subject matter. You know, of course, of the Diet of Worms?"

The children didn't, and Uncle Bill sighed. "Modern education," he said. "Million-dollar schools to produce five-cent minds. Ah, well. Actually, there were several diets, or meetings, held at the city of Worms in Saxony many hundreds of years ago. They were meetings of the learned men of Europe called to consider church matters, but at times the delegates talked of purely intellectual problems for their amusement. One of the problems on which they are supposed to have exercised their minds was 'How many angels can dance on the head of a pin?'

"Now to us moderns that seems like a ridiculous

question. Our minds are conditioned by the world in which we live, and unless we struggle against it, we fall into patterns of thought that are produced by the world around us. Listen carefully because what follows is important.

"We think in terms of the concrete—of matter which can be touched and which occupies space and has weight. We call these things 'real' and conclude that because of their 'reality' they are the only important things. Even in our reading we prefer nonfiction to fiction—fact to fancy, because we think fact has reality and fancy has none.

"Our ancestors took a different view. They did not divide fact from fancy, pronouncing one real and the other unreal. They believed, indeed they knew, that both fact and fancy have their own kind of reality, one being quite as real as the other. Their minds were not trapped by the seeable, feelable, weighable things around them. Their minds were much better developed than ours because they were less mechanical. They knew that an idea was just as real as a carving knife. So when they put to themselves the question, 'How many angels can dance on the head of a pin?' they were really asking, 'Does an angel (or an idea) occupy space?'

"If you don't believe in angels (and I hope you do), then what the learned gentlemen were debating at the Diet of Worms was how many ideas can be put on the head of a pin. If an idea is real, how much space does it occupy? How much does it weigh? And can it be put in a particular location—on the head of a pin or on the top of that stove like the pot?

"You see, what they were groping toward was a distinction between the spiritual and the material. But, unfortunately, the material world won the day. The nature of angels was abandoned and instead we got reinforced concrete, lath and plaster construction, contour plowing, automobiles, jet planes and rockets, and frozen vegetables. Not bad things at all, really. But we lost the angels. And that brings me to the little lights."

"Are *they* angels?" asked Patricia.

"No," said Uncle Bill. "They are not. But they are nonetheless beings, beings who have only recently found a means of getting to Earth, and more important, making themselves visible, for in their natural state they cannot be detected by the human eye, though they can be detected by the human brain."

"If they can be detected by the human brain," said Kevin, "why did they have to make themselves visible?"

"Because of the way in which the human brain has developed through the centuries," said Uncle Bill. "Our brains doubt the existence of anything that cannot be seen or measured or felt. That being the case, these creatures, though they could make an impression on the brain to signal their presence, were not believed since they were invisible. You yourselves, when you landed at the airstrip and did not know in what direction to walk, were told the direction by these creatures. Being children, you listened. Had you been adults, I am afraid you would have rejected the message because the bearer was invisible. Children are a little more inclined to believe in the reality of the unseen than grownups."

"What are the little lights called?" asked Arabella.

"Lumens," said Uncle Bill. "At least that is the name I have given to them. What they call themselves is quite incomprehensible to us because they communicate among themselves by means of a type of energy that we cannot detect. If *that* puzzles you, try to think of electricity as being a living creature and then try to think of electricity trying to tell you what it calls itself—not what we call it. It's the same thing with the lumens. We can't understand their language, so I have had to teach them ours. Morse code proved the best medium for communication. They are working on a better system themselves, involving manipulation of human brain cells so as to put in our minds the thoughts or information they want to convey. But there are complications."

"What kind of complications?" asked Christopher.

"Receptiveness of the individual," said Uncle Bill. "If the brain is otherwise occupied or rejects what they are trying to convey, they cannot get through. For a lumen to communicate with a human being, the human being has to be willing to receive a message. But let me get on with my story.

"The lumens come from a planet that is a satellite of Venus. It rotates around Venus as the moon rotates around the Earth. It is larger than the moon and has a heavy vegetation with beautiful fruits that I find superior to those of Earth. The mulpe, for instance."

"Mulpe?" said Kevin.

"The stuff you had with the pancakes. It comes from this planet, which is called Nede. When I say that it is called Nede, I mean that that is the word that the lumens put in my mind when I wanted to know the name of their planet. Because I am what is called highly receptive (as you yourselves may well prove to be), they can communicate directly with me merely by producing a series of brain waves that give me the information I require. They no longer have to be visible either. I can tell when they are about."

"Where are they now?" asked Arabella. "I want my teensy one back."

"Right here," said Uncle Bill. "I scolded them for making themselves visible to you, and they've been invisible ever since." The children looked and there, in the shadow of the mantelpiece above the fireplace, were the lumens. The little one came immediately to Arabella and settled on her nose.

"They're mischievous at times," said Uncle Bill. "Just think where you want Ita to be, and she will go there."

Arabella thought of her ear, and Ita became a little earring for her.

"How do you know their names?" asked Christopher.

"Just think," said Uncle Bill, and by doing this, the children got the names of several of the lumens and found that the chief of them was called Plutonius. He struck them as being kinder and wiser than the others, but a little disturbed, though they could not then understand the reason.

"Please go on, Uncle Bill," said Kevin. "And you kids be quiet. No more questions until the end. We won't get anywhere at this rate."

"Okay," said Uncle Bill. "Maybe later I will tell you in detail how living here alone, and engaged in what I'll have to call research into the theory of mathematics, I first began to suspect the presence of the lumens. You will have to be satisfied for the time being with the explanation that I thought of them first of all as hunches—suggested answers to problems which baffled my reason and which came to me unexpectedly and proved to be correct.

"I was working on the problem of infinity and trying to invent a mathematical language whose symbols would express time distance and speed as well as recurrence. . . . " He glanced at the children and saw by their faces that he had utterly lost them. "All right," he said. "I was working on some difficult problems and the answers came to me. Not just one answer or two answers, but a series of answers. I thought that this was the result of my subconscious continuing to work on the problems when I was asleep, but then I received a message, like a voice in my mind, saying, 'Why not from outside of you instead of from inside of you? Your own mind is limited and cannot contain the universe.'

"Now, I had done considerable reading in Tarki's

Elements of Human Perception and Understanding . . ." He looked at the children again and shrugged. "All right," he said. "Forget it. What I thought of as a hunch turned out to be Plutonius, and although I had difficulty in realizing that there could be creatures on the Earth other than those we can see, I finally concluded that this was so. The lumens are but the latest and best-adjusted to human intelligence."

"You mean there are others?" asked Kevin.

"Certainly," said Uncle Bill. "Creatures from Venus, from Uranus, from Jupiter, and even from unknown planets many light years away from us. We humans have been dimly aware of this for hundreds of thousands of years but never identified these beings. Where do you think the stories of goblins and water spirits and ghouls, common to every nation, come from? Fortunately, most of these creatures, though curious about Earth, are quite indifferent to human beings and are more fascinated by vegetable life than by human life. Some of them, including the dendrons, came originally from Mars and are very dull things that take up residence in trees here on Earth. They can be vicious-minded, but only when aroused.

"But to get back to my story. When I first suspected the existence of creatures who were communicating with my brain, I put the theory to a test and it checked out perfectly. I asked questions to which I did not then know the answers. I received the answers and then, independently, worked them out and found them correct. It is very clever of the lumens to realize that the human brain is stimulated by specific organs—the eye and the hand—and works best in cooperation with these. An eye to see and a hand to touch are very important tools of the human brain. When the lumens realized this, they contrived to make themselves luminous by a constant discharge of energy around them which causes a flamelike glow.

"Before they made themselves visible, there were times when the lumens could not get through to me because of unconscious resistance on my part. Even when I was convinced that I thoroughly believed in their presence, I was actually doubting it, and they could not produce the necessary brain waves to talk with me. That was when they realized that we have trained our brains to depend heavily on the evidence of the eye and the hand . . . very much less, by the way, than on the evidence of the nose and the ear, for we often doubt the sounds we hear or the scents that come to us.

"Anyway, they made themselves visible, and so we developed a Morse-code method of communicating until I could reverse the centuries of inherited training my brain had received in believing only what could be seen or felt. If more time had been spent on angels after the Diet of Worms, we would not now be the prisoners of our senses."

"So they told you that they came from Nede and they took you there in their flying saucer?" prompted Kevin, who didn't want to get wrapped up in the Diet of Worms and all that stuff again.

"Not *their* flying saucer, *mine*," said Uncle Bill, a little nettled. "They don't need a flying saucer to get there. They have no bodies. They can transfer themselves anywhere without mechanical means. But I, having a body that required protection, had to have a flying saucer, so I built one, and I use it for voyages to Nede, and other planets, too."

"What's it made of?" asked Christopher.

"Fiberglass," said Uncle Bill. "It's tough, slightly elastic, an excellent insulator against heat and cold and also against various rays encountered in space, and with a little skill you can put screws and nails into it to hang up clothes and cups and so on. The saucer shape, of course, not only is aerodynamic, to cope with the atmosphere of Earth and the slightly denser atmosphere of Nede, but also has enormous strength. An elephant could stand on two saucers exactly fitted one on top of the other."

"It's a very pretty pink," said Arabella, who sensed that Uncle Bill was a little touchy about his flying saucer.

"That's only the effect of the power supply in flight," he said.

"What do you use for power?" asked Christopher.

"Lumens," said Uncle Bill. "Two of them can put out sufficient power to get me to Nede. But, with you children on board, we may have to use three. And since we should start at five in the morning, you had all better get some sleep right now. The rest I will tell you later, or you will find out for yourselves."

"You mean we are going to Nede with you?" asked Patricia.

"In view of the fact that you know about the lumens and the flying saucer, I don't see any alternative," said Uncle Bill.

CHAPTER EIGHT

THE children slept until about four in the morning, rather surprised that they were able to sleep at all, for they were very excited. Uncle Bill got them sleeping bags for beds, and they stretched out in front of the kitchen fire and so spent the night. Ita awakened Arabella at four by telling her (after the manner of a lumen) that it was time to get up and to wake the others, which she did. All except Christopher. The three of them couldn't wake Christopher, but Plutonius finally got a strong message of some significance through to him and Christopher sat up and said in a very disgusted tone, "Ball Four. . . . I walked him." He was about to go to sleep again, but Kevin got him to his feet, and in a little while he was awake enough to realize that they must be moving.

Instructed by the lumens, who communicated by arranging the waves in their brains and indeed guided by their light, the children went out to the flying saucer, and on the way Kevin, thinking rather fearfully of

Venus and the tremendous distance that separated it from Earth, asked, "What about food? We are going to have to have enough for weeks, and what about telling Mom and Dad where we are going? Gosh, they'll really be worried."

Although this question was not addressed to anybody in particular, and indeed was not even spoken aloud, Plutonius answered it. "Don't countervibrate," he said. "Everything will be well."

"What do you mean by countervibrate?" asked Kevin. After a consultation among themselves and then a reference to Uncle Bill, Plutonius apologized and said that by countervibrating he meant worrying. He explained that he used the phrase because the effect of worry on the brain, as he perceived it, was a series of vibrations of different lengths interfering with each other and preventing a useful pattern of thought from developing.

Uncle Bill was already in the flying saucer checking that everything was secured for the take-off. When the children entered, they discovered that the saucer was divided into two compartments, one in the lower half and the other in the upper half. These compartments were connected by a spiral stairway of stainless steel or some other glittering metal. The lower compartment represented the sleeping quarters. It was bare of furniture, except for cupboards for clothing around the walls. The floor was of a rather stiff sponge rubber that was springy and very pleasant to walk on. There were a series of silvery rings set in this floor covering, with white straps attached to them.

"We will all sleep down here," said Uncle Bill. "And this is where you will stay for the take-off. The straps attached to those rings are to keep you down to the floor when you are sleeping. When we get into space, you will be almost weightless for a while. To stop yourselves drifting around the room while you are asleep, you must strap yourselves to the floor each night. But you will get accustomed to that."

"Do we have to strap ourselves down for the take-off?" asked Kevin.

"Yes. Actually, you couldn't move if you tried, because as a result of the acceleration your weight will be increased to several tons. But if the saucer were to tilt slightly you might be sent crashing with the weight of several tons against the side. So you have to be strapped down. The straps will hold you and you won't feel any real discomfort. Most of your discomfort will come from your imagination. If you can just accept the fact that nothing unpleasant will happen to you, you will suffer much less. Scared?"

"Yes," said Patricia. One of the lumens came to her. "My name is Una," the lumen said (by producing these words in Patricia's mind). "I will stay with you all the time, and then you won't be frightened. When we get to Nede, I'll stay with you and take you to the Seesuch, you and your sister and Ita and me."

"What's the Seesuch?" asked Patricia.

"You'll see," said Una. "It's lovely. Everything on Nede loves the Seesuch." Indeed, at the mention of the word all the lumens in the flying saucer glowed brighter with pleasure, and Uncle Bill, who had been a bit preoccupied and testy, smiled and said, "The Seesuch is almost as beautiful as the Vergroves."

"It's better," said all the lumens together, and little Ita, jumping up and down on the back of Arabella's hand, where she had taken up her position, kept crying, "It's much much better."

"Hush," said Plutonius. "De gustibus non est disputandum." And although Kevin had never done really well at his Latin in high school, he knew immediately that this meant "There is no accounting for tastes." So, as a matter of fact, did all the others, and they had never studied Latin. And that was most peculiar.

The upper compartment of the saucer was a large and lovely living-dining room. The floor was of the stiff sponge rubber. There was a large and handsome dining table in the center and chairs of the kind called Jacobean around it, equally handsome, chairs and table being bolted to the floor, as was everything else in the spacious compartment.

Around the bulkhead or circular wall that marked the limits of this compartment were set off the various work areas—kitchen, laundry area, food-storage area, a work desk, a series of filing cabinets, a navigation table and instruments for navigation, a photographic section, and a section devoted (to judge by brushes and boxes of paints, palette knives, palettes, and sculptor's chisels and hammers) to art.

"I didn't know you were an artist, Uncle Bill," said Kevin.

"You don't know that I'm an artist," said Uncle Bill. "The possession of the tools of an artist doesn't make a man an artist. You haven't seen any of my work, and so you don't know whether I am an artist or a mere dauber or fake."

"I didn't mean to offend," said Kevin, blushing at this rebuff.

"That's all right. My fault," said Uncle Bill. "I get impatient when people jump to conclusions on insufficient evidence. I'm just not used to having children around. That's what's the matter. It isn't that I don't like you. It's just that having children around is strange for me."

"That's okay," said Kevin. "If we can help you, let us know."

"Nothing more to be done but strap ourselves in down below," said Uncle Bill. "I can't explain all the things that are going to happen or we'll never get off. Just believe me when I say that you won't get hurt. And stop worrying. Goodness, I had to do this all by myself once, and nobody had ever done it before."

They went then to the lower compartment and strapped themselves down. Kevin saw that his sisters were secured and checked Christopher and then put his own straps on. Uncle Bill settled down beside him, secured his straps, and said, "All right, Plutonius. You take over. But whoever supplies the power, tell them to take it easy. This isn't Indianapolis." He turned to Kevin. "The lumens like manipulating the saucer," he said. "And some of them get too enthusiastic for my taste. When I want to break my neck, I'll do it myself, without help from these blinking lumens."

"Don't you like them?" asked Kevin.

"Certainly I like them," said Uncle Bill. "But that doesn't give them the right to break my neck. In any case, I can get just as angry with people I like as with people I don't like. There's no law against it."

"Ready for take-off," said Plutonius evenly. "Do you want a count down?"

"No," said Uncle Bill. "That kind of tomfoolery is strictly for television audiences. Just take off."

The first thing of which the children were aware was a very tiny buzzing sound, like a small fly trying to get through a window on a summer's day. At its loudest it was very small, and it quickly diminished to nothing. The children felt themselves sink into the sponge rubber as if being pressed gently and even with affection into it. And then Kevin tried to say something to Arabella to comfort her and discovered that he could not move his mouth and felt as though his eyes were stones that were trying to sink through his brain. But this feeling lasted only for a moment and was gone, and although they all remained incapable of movement for a while, they were drowsy rather than uncomfortable.

At the start the interior of the saucer had been lit by neon lights, but in a matter of a few seconds the exterior light was so bright that the neon tubes were quite useless. "We have risen from night into day," said Plutonius. "Down on the earth it is still night, but up here, a hundred miles high and far above the earth's horizon, it is daylight."

"Like the Rubaiyat of Omar Khayyam—FitzGerald's translation," said Uncle Bill.

" '*Awake! for Morning in the bowl of Night*
Has flung the Stone that puts the Stars to Flight . . .'

We being the stone in this instance. You know the Rubaiyat, of course?"

Kevin admitted that he didn't, which brought a snort from Uncle Bill. "Modern education," he said. "No Diet of Worms. No FitzGerald. They are not educating you, boy. What they are doing is killing you—committing spiritual murder on millions of children. What is the use of teaching children to read and giving them no poetry?

"Tremble Darkness. I, a little light,
Born of a hundred million hopes, approach."

"Who wrote that?" asked Kevin.

"I did," said Uncle Bill. "You can unstrap yourselves now and take a look out of the windows, and then we'll have breakfast." He turned to Patricia. "Your name is Patricia, isn't it?" he said.

"Yes."

"See," cried Uncle Bill, as if he had achieved an enormous triumph, "I am getting used to children already. And that is close to a miracle, for I have always abominated them. It is possible that by the time we are through with our present venture I may even be fond of you. There is one thing to be said in your favor immediately."

"What is that?" asked Christopher, undoing the last of his straps.

"The lumens like you. And they have excellent judgment, which is demonstrated by the fact that they like me. Well, take a look around, and then let's get on with breakfast. Can any of you make coffee?"

"I can," said Christopher.

"Fine, make me a pot. Three big spoonfuls, and use cold water. Get it on and then you can look out the windows." Christopher hurried to do this and then joined the others staring out into the blue and silver world that lay about and below them.

They were soaring, he found, above an azure floor which, like the flying saucer, was circular in shape. From this floor, fluffy mounds and pillars of cloud rose up, but as he watched they shrank smaller and smaller until, in a matter of only a few minutes, columns a mile high were hardly to be distinguished from the flatness below them. There were a few breaks in the clouds which

looked like dark holes into whose depths it was impossible to see. However, in one of these holes (which looked like the warrens of animals) they caught a glimpse of twinkling lights, as if the inhabitant possessed of a body that gave off dots of light was looking up at them. The sight was almost frightening.

"That's Honolulu," said Plutonius. "We are two hundred miles up but can still see the lights from some of the big places."

"Two hundred miles?" cried Arabella and grabbed the windowsill lest she fall.

"Don't worry," said Ita. "We lumens won't let you down," and the others chuckled.

"Soon," said Plutonius, "Earth will be only a blue globe clad in a garment of tattered silver. And then you will enter the great contradiction that lies at the bottom of all truth—the Dark Field of Lights."

"What does that mean?" asked Kevin. "I don't understand."

"In space there is no visible light," said Plutonius. "There is no atmosphere or gas to produce a diffusing and reflecting medium. All is black—blacker than anything you have ever seen. And yet in the blackness you will see the suns of the universe, beautiful, brilliant, and distant, scintillating all about you and lovelier than any sight Earth has to offer. So what you call space we call the Dark Field of Lights."

"Can *you* see light?" asked Christopher. "I mean, you haven't eyes, so how can you see things?"

"Eyes are only one instrument for sensing presence," said Plutonius. "There are many many others, possessed by different creatures. Light is a form of energy, a vibration, and so we can pick it up and analyze it and know what it is. We can analyze it so well that we can hear the sounds of light, which you cannot."

"You mean that a flame, like the flame of a candle, makes a noise?" asked Christopher.

"What you would call a noise—yes," replied Plutonius. "You can pick up only two of its vibrations—the light and the heat. We can pick up the sound as well, or really the choir of sounds, for it gives off not just one sound vibration but many."

"And that being the case, I can tell without looking at it that the Impatient Wise One's coffee is boiling," said a lumen who had remained close to Christopher since he boarded the saucer.

"Gee, thanks," said Chris, and went to take the coffee off the battery-operated electric stove. "What's your name?" he asked.

"Strike Three," replied the lumen.

"You're kidding," said Christopher.

"Yes. I am. But I know you like baseball and I want to be your friend and have a name that you will like. Since you're a pitcher, I thought Strike Three would sound best to you."

"It's a queer kind of a name," said Christopher. "But I kind of like it, all right."

"Fine," said the lumen. "Strike Three it will be. Just

think of the name and I'll be there. The Impatient Wise One likes his coffee with milk and sugar. Two teaspoonfuls of sugar, and I'll tell you when on the milk."

"Did you use to make it for him?" asked Christopher.

"No. We can't make anything. We have no bodies, and although we can supply energy to things—like to the motors of this flying saucer—we can't exert physical force by ourselves. For instance, I could tell you how to pitch a curve ball but I couldn't pick up the ball and throw it myself."

A thought occurred quite suddenly to Christopher. "Hey," he said, "were you running this saucer, I mean, supplying the energy to the controls, when you saw us in the airplane yesterday? And did you make it do that inside curve and slider combined?"

"Yes," said Strike Three, "I was. I was trying to signal you."

"What a pitch!" said Christopher. "If I had that in my bag of tricks, we'd get to the state finals."

"I can explain it," said Strike Three. "It's a matter of selecting a major axis at an angle of thirty-five degrees from the gravitational . . ."

"Where's that cup of coffee?" roared Uncle Bill. "Are you kids going to spend the rest of the voyage looking out the window, or do we get breakfast around here?"

CHAPTER NINE

THE journey to Nede took only three days or, since in space there is neither day nor night but only continuance (eternity as opposed to time), seventy-two hours measured by the electric clock on the space ship. The clock was more than a clock, for it kept the date as well, and the year also, for Uncle Bill said that he once spent eighteen months on Nede (measured by Earth time) and since his navigational method was based on the position in space of Earth, he had to know the month and the year as counted on Earth to arrive at its location.

"Otherwise I would have had some difficulties returning," he said. "I needed to take off when Earth and Venus were approaching each other and would continue to do so for some time. To take off when Earth was receding from Venus would involve a hazardous chase across space which only a fool would undertake."

At first there was so much to be seen that the children could hardly leave the observation windows. Saturn burned majestically in the sky with its magnificent rings, which Uncle Bill said were probably solid particles, millions of tiny little satellites circling the planet, some of them no bigger than baseballs.

"Are they made of rock, do you think?" asked Christopher.

"Probably not," said Uncle Bill. "Most likely they are solid chunks of ammonia, which, as you know, is chemically expressed as NH_3 and is a gas at normal temperatures but becomes a solid at minus 37 degrees Centigrade. Since the temperature on Saturn is about minus 150 degrees Centigrade, all the ammonia on Saturn must be solid."

The children stared at the planet, which, if they had seen it from Earth at all, had appeared as only a bright star of whose identity they were unconscious. Now it was smaller than when seen from Earth, because there was no atmosphere to magnify its size. But it was much sharper, its three principal bands of rings as clean-cut as the brim of a hat, and the planet itself glowing in a variety of colors, with shades of blue and green and yellow, but salmon pink predominately.

"A very interesting planet, Saturn," said Uncle Bill. "It makes such a wide orbit around the sun that it takes almost thirty years to complete its circle. That means that year after year it is almost in the same place in the sky. The Earth goes around the sun thirty times to Saturn's once, and using the two, with the sun as center, I have worked out a kind of calendar clock for use on

Nede. Earth is the minute hand and Saturn the hour hand, and with a little calculation I can work out the year and month, just in case that electric calendar clock should break down."

"Is Saturn solid like Earth?" asked Kevin.

"Can't say," said Uncle Bill. "It doesn't seem to be solid. It behaves as if it were a huge ball of liquid or of gas, or powder circling around the sun and spinning very quickly as it does so. It spins so quickly that a day on Saturn is not much more than ten Earth hours. But all the places on Saturn don't spin at the same speed, as they would if Saturn were solid. For instance, the areas around the equator spin a lot faster at times than the areas around the poles."

"Then it must be a gas or a liquid," said Kevin.

"No," said Uncle Bill. "We may not be seeing the surface. We may only be seeing a gas or liquid atmosphere around it. But the fact that Saturn is spinning so fast suggests that the rings around it may once have been big satellites, like our moon, which were spinning so rapidly that they exploded as a result of centrifugal force."

"Do you think there is life on Saturn?" asked Patricia.

It was Plutonius who replied. "There is life everywhere," he said. "Not the kind of life you would recognize because you are accustomed to a physical presence. But life, in one form or another, extends throughout the whole universe, some of it well developed, some of it primitive."

"Are there other beings on Nede besides yourselves?" asked Christopher.

"Yes. Many. Most of them have bodies, so you can see them readily. Some you will recognize in a vague, remembering sort of way."

"Like cats and little kittens?" asked Arabella.

"No. Like dragons and wyverns and cockatrices and basilisks, and unicorns and manticores and sea horses and mermaids and gorgons . . ."

"I'd sooner cats and little kittens," said Arabella.

"That's because you've never seen a baby gorgon," said Plutonius. And Ita started to jump up and down (this seemed to be a habit with Ita when excited or enthusiastic), piping, "Baby gorgons are the best. Baby gorgons are the best," until Una told her to stop it. But she promised to take Arabella to a place she knew where there was a nest of baby gorgons, "all lovely blue and spangling."

Saturn, of course, was not the only planet they could see. Clear of the wall of the Earth's horizon, they beheld other planets—Mercury, Mars, and Jupiter, and some of the smaller ones of which they knew nothing—Eros, Ceres, Adonis, and Hermes, for instance. These tiny planets, though so close to earth, were hard to pick out against the blaze of lights that surrounded them, all brilliant as diamonds held against a drape of black velvet. But they found where to look and how to look, and Uncle Bill, pointing out tiny Hermes, said the planet came so close to Earth that it passes between the moon and Earth and crosses the orbit of both Earth and Venus, diving in toward the sun before starting to swing wide again.

"Lucky it doesn't crash into Earth," said Christopher.

"Luck hasn't a thing to do with it," snorted Uncle Bill. "It's part of the Plan."

"What Plan?" asked Christopher. But Uncle Bill did not reply.

Venus they did not see until Earth itself had been reduced to the size, though not the shape, of a baseball, for Venus was at the time an evening star and thus behind the Earth when they took off just before dawn. Earth then became a blue sphere of a shade a little lighter than that of a forget-me-not, with the tracery of its green and gold continents just visible like a worn and faint arabesque on a shield of blue enamel. The clouds seemed not clouds any longer but a heavenly fabric spun out of pure light . . . and the whole sight an enchantment, silent and mystical.

From behind this lovely azure globe came Venus, tiny and shimmering, rising like a minute angel into the black night of the Heavens, and seeing it, the children gasped with awe and pleasure.

"It's so lovely, everyone on Earth should see it," said Patricia.

After watching Venus for a while, Christopher, puzzled, said, "Hey! Who's steering this thing?"

"The lumens, why?" said Uncle Bill.

"I hope they know what they're doing," said Christopher. "It seems to me that we should be heading for Venus instead of way off to the left of it."

"If we headed directly for Venus, we would make a big arc in the sky of hundreds of thousands of miles and wind up chasing it—and not catching it," said Uncle Bill. "We are headed out into space to a point where Venus will be in about fifty hours, when we will land on it . . . or rather on Nede, whose orbit is only a thousand miles above Venus."

"Fifty hours?" echoed Christopher. "Gosh, it's miles and miles to Venus. How fast does this thing go?"

"Through space and in round figures, about three and a half million miles an hour. Venus at the present time is only twenty-five million miles from us—closer than Mars by nine million miles. Of course, when we start entering the atmosphere of Venus, we will have to slow down to a mere five hundred miles an hour to avoid being destroyed by friction."

"And what about those little asteroid things that are supposed to be such a danger?" asked Kevin. "The things that are supposed to go clean through space ships like bullets?"

"Come over to the dark side of the flying saucer and you'll see," said Uncle Bill. The flying saucer had a dark side, of course, that portion of it which was away from the sun being in a shadow so deep as to seem almost solid. Looking out the windows of that side, they saw the saucer surrounded by flashes of light like hundreds of the brightest fireflies dancing about them.

"Gosh, are we on fire?" asked Kevin.

"No," said Uncle Bill. "I'm sure you've seen, in the fall of each year, a number of shooting stars in the night sky. As you know, those are asteroids or meteors which burn up on entering the Earth's atmosphere because of the friction induced by the tremendous speed at which they are traveling. Well, I have provided a slight atmosphere, no more than three feet deep, around the outside of the flying saucer. The tiny asteroids and meteorites of which you are talking burn up when they hit this atmosphere, and that is what you are seeing now. Those flashes of burning asteroids are taking place all around the flying saucer, but you can only see them on this dark side."

"I remember one of the early astronauts saying that he could see things like fireflies darting about in front of his sputnik," said Kevin.

"Yes," said Uncle Bill. "They were puzzled about that, and I wrote and gave them the explanation."

"What happened?" asked Kevin.

"They sent my letter back because of insufficient postage," said Uncle Bill. "I've let them struggle along by themselves with their space problems ever since."

CHAPTER TEN

By the time they were approaching Nede, the children knew a great deal about the planet and about Uncle Bill as well. They knew that Uncle Bill was going to Nede on an important errand, but what the errand was, they could not guess. The lumens could not tell them anything of it. Plutonius spent many hours of the journey with Uncle Bill, and after these talks Uncle Bill, or the Impatient Wise One, as the lumens called him, was always quiet and thoughtful for a while. The children learned not to talk to him until he, as if breaking a spell, spoke first. Before they discovered this, they were met, when they spoke to him, with an unseeing stare that was quite frightening.

Plainly then, all was not well on Nede, and Kevin suspected that some kind of an invasion was pending, perhaps from Venus, though the lumens spoke of Venus without any fear—all except Plutonius. He, when not engaged with Uncle Bill, attached himself to Kevin. Plutonius seemed to have a greater depth of mind than his fellow lumens, and although he was prepared to discuss Venus with Kevin, it was always with a touch of reluctance, as if there was on the planet something that he was loath to reveal.

From Plutonius, Kevin learned that Venus was almost entirely covered by water. There were several land masses, forming immense islands on the planet, but the proportion of land to water was far less than on Earth. Also, the land was very different, for it consisted either of towering mountains with sides so steep as to be unscalable, and on which nothing whatever grew, or immense boglands, which were thick with rushes, lily pads, with mangrove, giant golden grass, scarlet iris, and other waterland plants, some of which would be familiar to him and others completely strange.

The rains of Venus, Plutonius said, were like nothing on Earth. They were sudden and catastrophic, beating down so heavily that all creatures had to take shelter from them. "The rains of Venus roar like high-pressure steam escaping through a pipe," said Plutonius. "The sound would be deafening to you. You would be unable to see in the deluge and would be beaten to the ground by the heaviness of the cloudbursts and perhaps drowned. On Earth, three or four inches of rain in one storm is reckoned a deluge. On Venus, four inches of rain falling in an hour is thought only a shower."

"How can plants survive such a rain?" asked Kevin.

"They have adapted themselves to it," said Plutonius. "At first every scrap of vegetation is beaten by the pelting drops as if caught in a hail of stones. But in a matter of minutes so much water falls that the level of the water in the boglands rises. Lily pads, water weeds, bog grass—all the low-lying plants are soon underwater and so protected from the pelting of the rain.

"The taller plants, the rushes and sedges, are knocked down in the first few minutes. But again the water protects them as it rises, and when the rain is over, you will see all the plants rising in their thousands from the flooded bog. The sun comes out, hot as a furnace, the whole landscape steams and is covered by a writhing golden mist that forms quickly into purple clouds in the flame-red sky, and then, after a little while, comes the rain again."

"Flame-red sky?" echoed Kevin.

"Of course," said Plutonius. "The gas molecules in the atmosphere are infinitesimal in size. But the atmosphere of Venus is heavily charged with moisture, and each molecule is enlarged by droplets of water clinging to it. If you had not been the victim of a modern education (as the Impatient Wise One would say), you would know that enlarged molecules transmit or diffuse the lower end of the light spectrum—the reds and oranges. Which is the reason that Earth's sunsets are often a flaming red."

"I hope you are not going to start in on modern education, like Uncle Bill," said Kevin.

"I was joking," said Plutonius.

"Are there animals and other creatures living on Venus?" asked Kevin.

"Yes," said Plutonius, but in such a way as to suggest that he did not want to discuss this topic further.

"Many?"

"Not as many as on Nede."

"Is there a king or some kind of a ruler?"

"Yes."

"What is his name? What is he like?"

To this question, Plutonius would not reply. Kevin, however, returned to it many times, and in the end, having put the question to Plutonius once more, he received the impression of a huge glittering reptile emerging from a bowl of emerald the size of a house, and he heard or thought he heard the word, "Ka." The fancy or vision, whichever it was, frightened him. Then the dream or impression was gone, and he found Plutonius beside him.

"What happened to me" asked Kevin. "Have I been dreaming? Did I fall asleep?"

"You have been away," said Plutonius. "Where did you go?"

"I had a horrible kind of a nightmare," said Kevin.

"You traveled," said Plutonius. "Where did you go? What did you see?"

"I don't know where I was," said Kevin. "But there was a big green bowl—a huge thing. And out of it came this tremendous snake, all glittering like a jewel and moving very slowly."

"Ka," said Plutonius. "You have been to Venus and seen Ka, the Smiler. Did he speak to you?"

"No. I woke up. Surely it was only a dream."

"It was what you humans call a dream," said Plutonius.

"But it wasn't real, was it?" persisted Kevin.

"Everything is real," said Plutonius. "There are no unrealities."

"Tell me," said Kevin, after a little silence. "Is Ka real?"

"He is more than what you mean by real," said Plutonius. "He is eternal. He is indestructible. You cannot cut his head off with the sharpest sword."

"He terrified me," said Kevin.

"Then you are safe," said Plutonius. "When you stop being frightened of Ka, then you will be in danger. When you see him smile and feel sorry for him, that is the time to beware of Ka."

"Is it because of Ka that Uncle Bill is going to Nede?" asked Kevin. But to this question he received no answer from Plutonius.

They did not have to strap themselves down for the landing on Nede, but this was the result of the thoughtfulness of Plutonius, for Uncle Bill, preoccupied with his plans, would scarcely have thought of it. The chief lumen suggested that the flying saucer start decelerating when it was seven million miles from Venus and its satellite, so that the slowing down could take place over a period of two hours and thus be less uncomfortable.

Plutonius knew that both Arabella and Patricia were scared of the landing, and he wanted to ease it for them.

"Oh, all right," said Uncle Bill, irritated. "This is the result of space traveling with a kindergarten, I suppose." He pulled a slide rule out of his vest pocket and went through a quick calculation. "That will delay our arrival by one hour, forty-seven minutes, and thirteen seconds," he said.

"In space travel, time doesn't really matter, Impatient Wise One," said Plutonius.

"You can leave out that stuff about Impatient Wise One and just call me Captain," snarled Uncle Bill. "I have as much patience as anybody. In fact, I dare say that when it comes to patience, I could wear out Job, if there was any sense to it. Actually, Job would have been better off to have taken the heads of some of his so-called comforters and knocked them together until they rang like bells. What I haven't got patience with is waiting when there isn't any sense to waiting."

"That's right," said Arabella. "It's silly to wait for something when you don't have to."

"What a delightfully bright and intelligent child you are," said Uncle Bill. "Your name is Arabella, isn't it? See. I remembered." This really wasn't either a great feat or a compliment to Arabella, since the two had now been almost three days together, but Uncle Bill sounded very pleased with himself.

"Yes," said Arabella. "My name is Arabella and yours

is Uncle Bill . . . I think." For a moment he glared at her and then he laughed.

"Well," he said, "I suppose it really isn't very clever of me to remember your name. But, after all, I'm just not used to children or to thinking about children, and up to the present, one child hasn't meant any more to me than another. Just nuisances. That was all."

"You might try picking her up, Impatient Wise One," said Plutonius.

"If you had a head, I'd knock it against the wall," said Uncle Bill. But he did bend down and pick Arabella up, holding her as if she were made of very thin glass.

"There," said Plutonius. "That didn't hurt."

"Of course it didn't hurt," said Uncle Bill, who had rather liked it himself. "Never said it would. But I can't spend all day and all night picking up children and putting them down again. There are other things to be done. And the others are too big."

"I'm too heavy," said Kevin, who in fact weighed a good hundred and sixty pounds.

"Nonsense," said Uncle Bill. "I could pick up you and your brother. Here. Both of you sit on the floor and hold on to a forearm each." They did so, and Uncle Bill, breathing in slowly as he did so and thus expanding his chest, lifted them clear off the floor.

"Gosh, you really are strong," said Christopher.

"Of course I am," said Uncle Bill. "And I'll tell you the secret."

"He has been eating the fruits of Nede," said Plutonius.

"Nonsense," said Uncle Bill. "I always lived a good clean life, took plenty of fresh air and exercise, got up before dawn and went to bed . . ." But he never got through with that, for the lumens were flashing and hopping around the place as if in paroxysms of laughter, so he finished and said, "Well, let's cut out the carnival. We have to bring this thing in and get it down on the ground."

There was no difficulty to the landing. Venus for a long time seemed no bigger than when they had set out. Then it commenced to grow, increasing from a mere dot to a spot the size of a matchhead and then of a pea and then of a ball and changing from glittering cold silver to the faintest tint of blue, which became deeper and deeper the nearer they got.

When Venus was the size of the full moon, viewed from Earth, they first saw Nede, the satellite to which they were bound. It showed as a globe the size of an apple radiating a golden light against the blue of Venus. But these colors lasted only for a while. The blue became lighter and then became silver, and the gold of Nede paled to platinum and then turned to the palest of greens and then showed green and pink and white.

As they came nearer and nearer, Nede swelled like a balloon until it was almost the size of Venus and then, swelling even more monstrously, became so huge that Venus disappeared behind it.

A little later the satellite occupied the whole window through which they were looking, and then individual features began to appear on it—a huge tract of what appeared to be forest, except that the vegetation instead of being green was silver and blue; then an enormous area of purest blue, slashed with silver bands that ran here and there in a variety of patterns; then a plain or a prairie that was all gold and black in lovely patterns; and then an area of scarlet and white, the two colors seeming to perform a dance together, for parts that were scarlet swayed and became white and parts that were white, swaying likewise, became scarlet.

Right after flying over this area, Uncle Bill said to Plutonius, "Turn round and head for the Seesuch by Mantinal. We will land there and find out what has been taking place whilc you were away."

"You are indeed wise," said Plutonius. "Mantinal at this time is on the other side from Venus. It will not be known that we are back. Unless . . ."

"Never mind about unless," said Uncle Bill gruffly. "We'll get the facts and go from there. 'Unless' is a waste of time."

They swooped out over the area where the dance (it seemed a waltz) of the scarlet and white was being performed, and came again over the place of intense blue slashed with silver bands. Down and down they slipped toward this, and then the children saw that they were heading down to an ocean with a blue so deep that it seemed that the sky had fallen to the land. There were large waves rolling nobly over the surface of the ocean, some of them as high as hills, and their clifflike tops broke into cascades of glittering silver.

Down, down they went, and then, in a terrible second, the flying saucer plunged into the sea, and the light of Nede, which had a slight rosebud-pink tinge, was turned to deep blue, for they were underwater.

"We've crashed," cried Patricia.

"We'll drown," cried Arabella.

But the lumens only laughed. "Nobody ever drowned in the Seesuch," said Una. "It's the happiest place in Nede. You'll see. And it's the safest, too. No harm can come to us there."

"Harm," thought Kevin, and remembered Ka and wondered if the occupant of the huge emerald bowl was even then searching for them.

CHAPTER ELEVEN

THE children thought that the flying saucer, having plunged (though without the slightest shock) below the surface of the Seesuch or Neden Ocean, would after a little while surface again, but this was not so. It continued on down, the increase in depth being marked by only the slightest deepening of the lovely blue about them. Silver bubbles trailed past them, as gay as sprites, and they went through a thicket of golden kelp on which hung little balls of purple color in clusters, like grapes.

On the other side, they settled to the bottom, which was pale gold but beautifully mottled with light and shadow from the reflection of the sun through the surface of the water. The bottom, then, was like a living thing, full of color and of movement, and enormously inviting.

Here the flying saucer stopped for the first time since leaving Coppertown. Everybody had gathered in the upper compartment, but Uncle Bill now led the way down the glittering stainless-steel circular staircase below. Here the air was a deeper and indeed a prettier blue than in the upper compartment, for not quite as much surface light was present.

"I feel just as if I was in the bottom of a lovely swimming pool," said Arabella.

"It's so quiet," said Patricia. "So peaceful." And so it was, like being in a huge and noble cathedral or a grove of lofty forest trees, their branches so high that not even the faintest rustling of the leaves could be heard.

"I feel really safe," said Arabella, and Kevin had that feeling, too, of finding the way back to a lovely and wonderful place, lost long long years ago. When he was much smaller, his father had taken him to New England to a farm. There one day, with Christopher, he had found a thick growth of hazel bushes and, pushing aside the branches, had crawled in, to find himself in a beautiful little house whose delicate green walls were made of the leaves of the nut trees, protecting and embracing him at the same time. The feeling of bliss and ease, which he had known then, returned to him now.

"Well," said Uncle Bill. "I could do with a little rest. Let's go outside and refresh ourselves."

"But it's water," said Patricia. "We'll drown."

"It's so lovely, I don't care if we do," said Arabella.

"You cannot be hurt by the water of Nede," said Uncle Bill. "Come. I'll show you."

He opened the hatch through which they had entered the flying saucer. Kevin moved Arabella and Patricia aside and called to Christopher to step back. He expected that when the hatch was open, the water would flood the flying saucer to a depth of four or five feet until the pressure inside and outside was equal. But nothing of the sort happened. The water did enter the saucer but welled up only a little way and then stopped.

The entrance of the water into the flying saucer was entrancing. It was as if when Uncle Bill removed the hatch it was to reveal underneath a beautiful blue jewel the size of the hatchway, and this, undulating with light, slowly grew until it had doubled its size as the water entered the compartment.

"Oh! How beautiful," said Patricia.

"Who wants to be the first to swim in the water of Nede?" asked Uncle Bill.

"Me," said Patricia.

"No, you don't," said Kevin. "You stay here until I try." He turned to Uncle Bill. "How deep down are we? I can skin-dive about thirty feet with fins, but not much more."

"We're about fifty feet down, and the bottom is twenty feet below us," said Uncle Bill. "But don't worry. And don't bother holding your breath. Just breathe the water."

"You crazy?" asked Kevin.

"No. You will find that you can breathe the water as readily as you can breathe the air. It is super-saturated with oxygen. You may sneeze a little to start with, but after that, you will have no trouble."

"You want to do it first to show me?" asked Kevin, who sensibly had a tendency to caution.

"No," said Uncle Bill. "I don't. Some things you are going to have to try out for yourself, so you might as well start."

Kevin stripped down to his shorts and cautiously put a toe in the gleaming blue jewel. Christopher laughed. "That's how the hope of the Dewey Weber surf team enters the water," he said.

"Feels great," said Kevin, submerging his foot. "Just right," he added, lowering himself to the shoulders and supporting his head above the water with his hands on the lip of the hatchway. "Gee. This water is terrific. Waikiki is cold mud compared with this. Man. This is the best ever."

"Okay," said Uncle Bill. "Let go. Put your head under and breathe."

"It doesn't feel that great," said Kevin. "Give me a line so you can pull me back if I get into trouble."

"Not necessary," said Uncle Bill. "You can see as clearly under the water as you can in the air."

"Without a face plate?" asked Kevin.

"Without a face plate."

"I still want a line," said Kevin, and Plutonius said, "One day Kevin may be as wise as his uncle. He doesn't rush into things."

"Bah," said Uncle Bill. "When we landed here the first time, Plutonius, you told me to open the hatch. I did. You told me to go in and breathe the water, and

I went in and breathed the water, without a line or a lot of palaver about it."

"That is true," said Plutonius. "But not many are like you, and that is what makes you impatient. Give the boy a line. It will reassure him and do no harm."

"Oh, all right," said Uncle Bill, and got a length of line and gave one end of it to Kevin.

"Hold the other end tight, Uncle Bill," said Kevin.

"Be careful," said Patricia. "Be careful about breathing that water."

"Oh, hurry up," said Arabella. "Ita and I want to get in, too. You're holding up everybody."

At this, Kevin took a great gulp of air and then submerged. They saw him kick down from the flying saucer, his hair (which was longish) streaming backwards in the water, his arms and legs moving easily and powerfully as he swam away from them, one hand, however, still holding the line. He had soon gone quite a way, and Patricia said, "He's going too far. He ought to come back. Pull him in, Uncle Bill."

Christopher was anxious too, and Uncle Bill, to reassure the children, stopped letting the line slip and took a couple of turns of it around his hand. Kevin, finding himself brought up short on the line, turned and seemed surprised to find the flying saucer already so far away. But he was not unhappy. He waved to them, and then a cloud of bubbles swarmed around his head and disappeared toward the surface.

"He just breathed out the last air in his lungs," said Uncle Bill. "Now he will have to breathe the water."

They watched and saw Kevin's chest expand slightly. He gagged or coughed a little, put his hand to his nose, and then looked up at them and smiled, and, putting thumb and forefinger together to form a circle, signaled the others, "O.K."

Then he gave a tremendous jerk of the line, and Uncle Bill, clothes and all, disappeared in an explosion of silver and blue through the hatchway. Kevin dropped the line immediately and fled with Uncle Bill behind him, his beard trailing from his chin with considerable grace and his bent, curved stem pipe still in his mouth.

The lumens were rolling around the floor, as it were, laughing, including the sober Plutonius, and Arabella piped, "Me next," and jumped in, clothes and all, to be followed by Patricia and Christopher, though Christopher stripped down to his shorts.

The water was slightly cold—its temperature being somewhere in the area that borders between cool and a touch of coldness. In short, it was just right—invigorating, and it sent the blood tingling through their veins. It was astonishingly clear, so that the children got the feeling that they were swimming or flying through the sky, way up beyond the clouds and the dust of Earth. And yet the silver carpet of the bottom, with its dappling of gold and purple and of palest pink, was only a few feet below them.

Patricia decided to try breathing the water right

away, before she was too far from the hatchway of the flying saucer, and did so. She felt a little catch in her chest as she took the water. And then she was breathing as naturally as she had breathed the air of Earth. Arabella didn't even think about it. She was so excited that she just went on breathing and so didn't experience a thing.

Christopher, however, sneezed, and his sneeze had a remarkable effect. He was immediately surrounded by an enormous school of small red fish, rather corpulent, with large eyes and puffed-out cheeks. Some pulled his eyelids down to stare at the area of the eyeball thus revealed; others clustered around his chest, the sides of their heads pressed against him as if listening to his heartbeat; others peered into his ears, jostling each other aside importantly to get a better view; and others poked a fin into his mouth and looked patient and thoughtful, as if taking his temperature.

"They think he's hurt," said Patricia, surprised and a little frightened to see her brother the center of attention of such a swarm.

"They're surgeon fish," said Una. "If they think anything in the Seesuch is hurt, they rush immediately to help."

"Cripes," said Christopher through a mouthful of tiny inquiring fins, "what do I do to get rid of them?"

"Just wait," said Strike Three. "When they're satisfied, they will go away."

It was quite a while before the surgeon fish were

satisfied. When they discovered that there was nothing the matter with Christopher (he had sneezed only because the temperature change had irritated his nasal passages), they went off to one side and held quite a convention, discussing his astonishing symptom, which seemed to be beyond all their medical experience. Then two of them detached themselves from the gathering and came to Strike Three and emitted a series of squeaks rather like the twitterings of bats.

"Open your mouth," said Strike Three. "They want to go inside and see where the sneeze came from."

"Do I have to?" asked Christopher.

"Oh, come on," said Strike Three. "They've never heard a sneeze before, and it's very exciting for them. Nothing ever happens to anybody here in the Seesuch, and they haven't a thing to do, so you will give them something to think about and discuss and evolve all kinds of theories around for a long time to come."

Christopher opened his mouth, and the two surgeon fish (first of all shaking fins in quite a heroic manner, like two explorers shaking hands before venturing into some appalling cavern) swam inside. It was unfortunate for them that one, turning to go out, touched the top of Christopher's mouth with its dorsal fin, producing a sneeze of Goliath proportions. The two little fish were flung out in a kind of whirlwind, and Christopher was immediately lost in such a swarm of them, all rushing to his assistance, that not a particle of him could be seen by his two sisters.

He might have remained lost for a long time, had not Uncle Bill returned with Kevin. He still had his pipe in his mouth, and catching sight of the multitude of surgeon fish, he made a curious noise, like someone clucking to a horse. Immediately the busy, fussy little fish left Christopher and, with a great deal of scurrying (like schoolchildren trying to get back to their desks at the approach of their teacher), formed themselves neatly into a series of rows before him. Uncle Bill then squeaked a little more, not even bothering to take his pipe out of his mouth, and the surgeon fish drifted off, so that in a moment not one was to be seen.

"What did you tell them, Uncle Bill?" asked Christopher.

"I told them to scram," said Uncle Bill. "I told them I'd take care of everything and explain it all to them later. What did you do?"

"Sneezed," said Christopher.

"Twice," said Arabella.

"Congratulations," said Uncle Bill. "Well. No harm done. You kids go off and explore. I have some things I have to do and some creatures I have to talk to."

"May I go with them?" asked Plutonius.

"Yes," said Uncle Bill. "I won't need you lumens for a while. See that they don't go too far. Remember that mortals take time to travel, unlike you lumens. Bring them back before dark."

This request surprised Strike Three, and although all

the lumens were remarkably respectful to Uncle Bill, he said, "Why must they be back before dark?"

"Because there is something they know of that I don't want you to learn about yet," said Uncle Bill.

"What is the name of this thing?" asked Strike Three.

"Its name is fear," said Uncle Bill.

CHAPTER TWELVE

TRAILING garlands of silver bubbles that appeared with the slightest movement, the children swam off through the blue water of the Neden sea with the lumens leading the way. Swimming they found was effortless. They scarcely needed to move their hands and arms but could make all the progress they wanted by just moving their legs, scissors fashion.

When they tired of that and wanted a change, they found they could fly through the water, using hands and arms as wings, and having picked up a little speed, could soar, like a seagull in the sky, on extended arms. They could do inside rolls and outside rolls and barrel rolls and any kind of maneuver they wanted, and this complete freedom of movement was such a delight in itself that for quite a while they did nothing but hold a kind of swimming circus (or perhaps flying circus would be a better phrase) in the crystal-blue water, flying in and out across each other's paths and playing tag.

Then tiring a little of this, Kevin called, "Come on,"

and headed for a rock that was off to one side and was the flaming red of a fire engine. It was perhaps fifteen feet high, coming up to a rough point, and apart from its spectacular color, not very much different from the seashore rocks of earth. "Touch it," said Plutonius, and Kevin did so. Immediately the whole rock changed its color from brilliant scarlet to silver.

"It's alive," said Patricia.

"What makes it do that?" asked Christopher, screwing his eyes in his inquiring way.

"Touch it again," said Strike Three.

Christopher did so, and the rock disappeared. At least they thought it had disappeared, but when Christopher, astounded, reached out to where the rock had been standing, his hand touched it once more, though he could not see it, and the rock sprang back into view fire-engine red again.

"It's a hiding-place rock," said Plutonius. "It is bright scarlet so that everyone can see where it is, but as soon as it is touched it takes on the color of the creature who touched it, thinking that a camouflage is needed."

"Silver," said Kevin. "I'm not silver."

"Well, that's the nearest it can come to the color of your skin without practice," said Plutonius. "If it could study you for a while, it would do better. But when Christopher touched the rock again, it turned the exact color of the water and so disappeared. He could then have gone behind it and been hidden if he were hiding from something."

"Hiding from what?" asked Christopher, giving a cautious look around.

"Hiding like when you are playing a game," said Strike Three. "What else?" He sounded genuinely surprised at the notion of hiding except in a game.

Arabella had not been listening to this conversation. She and Ita had been experimenting with the hiding rock. She found a black shell and touched it with that and it turned black. Then she found a white shell and it turned white. Then she touched it at the same time with both the white shell and the black shell, and it covered itself with large black and white squares like a crossword puzzle. The rock decided that that was wrong, though, and made black and white bands across itself. Then it altered the bands so that they ran vertically instead of horizontally. And then, seemingly in complete confusion, it disappeared, leaving Arabella and Ita in stitches.

But the rock had its revenge. When they started swimming again, though they set off in a different direction, Arabella immediately bumped into the hiding-place rock.

"I forgot to tell you they can move about when they're invisible," said Ita. Rubbing her nose, Arabella caught up with the others. They passed first of all a forest of golden kelp that was like a grove of tall gleaming trees, the leaves of beaten bronze and the trunks and branches of pale yellow. The leaves were huge, so big in fact that all four children could lie down on one, with plenty of room to spare. When they lay on it, the leaf rose and fell with a motion so gentle and comforting that they were almost put to sleep. These beautiful growths had bunches of fruit that looked like purple grapes, about the size of plums.

"Can we eat them?" asked Patricia.

"Yes," said Una, "but . . ." The sentence was not finished.

"But what?" asked Patricia.

"Go ahead," said Strike Three.

"If there's a but involved, I don't want any," said Patricia.

"Phooey," said Arabella. "I don't care about buts," and plucking one of the fruits, she took a big bite out of it before Ita could stop her. Immediately her eyes closed and she fell asleep, snoring quite prettily.

"Oh, bother," said Patricia. "That's spoiled everything. When Arabella goes to sleep, nothing will wake her. She's worse than Christopher." But tiny Ita took a piece of the leaf of the kelp tree and rubbed it on Arabella's lips, and she woke immediately and said, "Pancho is chasing his tail. He doesn't miss me at all, and Daddy's got some beautiful sweet peas growing all over the front of the house. Red and blue and white and pink."

"You've been dreaming," said Patricia.

"I have not been dreaming," said Arabella. "I was there and saw it."

"It is the same thing," said Plutonius. "What you

humans call dreaming is a kind of journeying. Because you have bodies, you think you are traveling only when your body accompanies your mind. But it is the mind that really travels, and it does not need the body with it.

"The fruit Arabella ate is the Fruit of Journeys. It can take you to the place most on your mind, whether you are consciously aware of the place or not. But you must always have a friend by you with some of the leaf to bring you back. The Fruit of Journeys can take you to some terrible places. It should not be eaten lightly. Una should not have allowed the child to eat it."

Una's light dimmed under this rebuke, but Strike Three said, "Surely it is safe for the children to eat this fruit. They could not be taken to anywhere terrible because their minds are not conscious of such places."

"Even we lumens do not understand the human mind," said Plutonius. "It is not created anew in each individual and free of all marks like a sheet of clean paper. It contains millions of waiting memories and desires and a huge deposit of knowledge passed on through a hundred thousand generations. Given the right signal, any one of these memories or desires will spring immediately into the conscious mind. The human mind loses nothing through the passing of the centuries, but constantly gains more. It is the most powerful and most fearful instrument in all the universe. Humans should eat of the Fruit of Journeys only deliberately—never lightly."

"Well, Pancho is fine," said Arabella, "and the sweet peas are really lovely. And I wasn't dreaming."

When they had got through the forest in which the Fruit of Journeys grew, they came to a huge and shining cliff of many colors. It soared high above them, for the Seesuch was much deeper here and sparkled in the light. It was of a thousand colors, as if its face was covered with millions of pieces of different colored glass or with millions of jewels. Parts of it looked like the inside of a pomegranate, being covered with ruby beads; other parts were faced with emerald icicles cascading down the side. Others were covered with diamond-shaped tiles of gleaming ebony, and other places were encrusted with azure crystals—in clusters like rock candy.

The face of this cliff was not straight but contained many headlands and caves and arches like flying buttresses jutting out from it, and the children explored this kaleidoscope of a cliff, delighted by the shapes and the colors. It looked so good that Patricia broke off an emerald icicle and put it in her mouth and found that it tasted like a Popsicle, only much, much better.

Also, the icicle never diminished, however much she sucked on it, and when she had had enough and threw it away, it floated back to its fellows and reattached itself to the cliff. Everything, they found, could be eaten, and everything had a different taste. But eaten is not the correct word, for the little rubies or the pieces of jet or the blue rock candy crystals never got smaller, and when finished with, returned to the cliff.

The lumens watched the children breaking off pieces here and there in deep interest, as if waiting for something to happen. And then Christopher, who had found a cluster of delicious-looking gold and purple rings, said, as he was about to put one to his mouth, "Hey, you guys. Listen. Do you hear anything?"

They all listened, and Kevin said, "Yes. Music. There's an orchestra somewhere around here. It is very faint and yet I can hear every note distinctly."

"Do you recognize any of the instruments?" asked Plutonius.

"I think there's a harp—only much better," said Christopher.

"And violins," said Kevin.

"And a flute, or maybe it is someone singing," said Patricia.

"And a big old drum," said Arabella. They listened intently, but the faint, yet distinct tones of the orchestra gradually died away.

"It came from over there," said Kevin. "Behind that big green ridge. Let's go." Off they went, reached the emerald ridge jutting out from the face of the cliff, swam over it, and found beyond a kind of amphitheater, the floor covered with white sand, and something else that made them gasp.

"Mermaids," cried Christopher. And that is what they were—seven of them, sitting around on rocks, each with an instrument on which she had been playing. They looked up at the children without fear or surprise, as if the children were not strangers but creatures they were accustomed to seeing every day.

"We were wondering if you would hear them," said Una to Patricia. "We wanted you to, but we were not sure that you would."

"'They were very faint," said Christopher.

"Yes, but the big thing is that you *did* hear them," said Strike Three. "The Impatient Wise One never has. He knows they are here because we have told him so. But he has never heard them or seen them."

"Why?"

"We don't know," said Strike Three. "It is one of the things about him that puzzles us."

"Can they speak?" asked Kevin.

"Yes," said Plutonius. "Perhaps they will talk to you. Once there were many of them on your planet, Earth, in the days when Greece was the greatest of your nations. Even then, however, not many could hear them, and before they can be seen by humans, they must first of all be heard. Those who did hear them were often so fascinated by the music that they forgot to manage their ships properly and their ships were broken up on the rocks on which the mermaids gathered to sing and play. They were called sirens, at that time."

"Ulysses was afraid of them," said Kevin.

"That's right," said Plutonius. "And rightly."

"And what about us?" asked Kevin. "Will we be unable to leave if they play again? If not, let's get out of here."

"You need not be afraid, because no harm can come to you here," said Plutonius. But Kevin was nervous because, although the mermaids were beautiful, they looked at him and his brother and sisters with unseeing eyes that contained no warmth or welcome.

"What are they thinking of?" whispered Patricia.

"Perhaps of Earth, where they once lived," said Plutonius.

"Can't you ask them?" Patricia persisted. "I don't like the way they look."

"I will ask them, and they will speak to you," said Plutonius, and did so. And this is what the children heard.

"Children of another place,
Fair of limb and fair of face,
Voyagers through space and time,
See, we mourn the fall of Priam,
Mourn for Troy and Ulysses,
Mourn for Scylla, Charybdis;
Mourn oars that struck a wine-dark sea,
Last memories of Greece are we."

And then, taking up their instruments, they sang beautifully and sadly of ancient times.

CHAPTER THIRTEEN

WHEN the mermaids had finished their song, Patricia felt sorry for them and thanked them. She wished she had some gift to give them, but all she could think of was a hair band of imitation horn with some paste jewelry in it which came from a five-and-ten-cent store. Still, deeming it better than nothing, she took this from her hair and gave it to one of the mermaids, who she hoped was the principal of the group, and Arabella added a ring of which she was very fond.

She was not quite as bashful as Patricia, being younger, and she took the mermaid's hand and put the ring on one of her fingers and told her that it had a piece of real imitation coral in it and had cost twenty-five cents and the labels off three cans of cat food.

The mermaid, with a kind of sad pleasure, smiled at these gifts, and taking up her harp, sang a little song of thanks:

"Little maids with gifts so rare,
One for hand and one for hair,

My name you'll find writ in the stars,
The jewel that mocks at mighty Mars.
Call to me if you should be
In need of aid in any sea."

The children then left the mermaids, and Patricia said to Una, "I wonder what her name could be? I'll never guess it—'The jewel that mocks at mighty Mars.' This doesn't mean anything to me."

"Me neither," said Una. "Sometimes we lumens come and listen to the mermaids, hoping to learn something from them of their time on earth. But they never sing the same song twice and they talk of so many gods and goddesses and heroes that it confuses even us. Plutonius might know because he is more advanced than the rest of us. Ask him." But Plutonius replied that the mermaid had intended Patricia and Arabella to find out her name for themselves, and it would not be fair for him to help. But he said it might be all right if they asked Uncle Bill.

"Maybe it's Hershey," said Arabella.

"Why Hershey?" asked Patricia.

"Well, Hershey bars are kind of rivals of Mars bars," said Arabella.

"Oh, nuts," said Kevin. "Can you imagine a mermaid being called Hershey?"

"Well, they taste good," said Arabella, who when she had a point defended it to the last and from any position that offered.

Arabella then remembered something they had been promised on the journey from Earth and asked, "Can we see the nest of baby gorgons now?"

"Yes," said Una, very pleased with the suggestion. "Let's go." But Plutonius said they couldn't.

"They are too far away," he said. "There isn't time for the children to swim there."

"How far away are they?" asked Kevin.

Plutonius did not reply immediately, being, it seemed, engaged in some kind of calculation. Then he said, "Twenty-three miles, five furlongs, and three rods, perches, or poles."

"Whatever *they* may be," said Christopher.

"Aren't those measurements from Earth?" asked Plutonius, a little taken aback. "I'm sure they are, for I learned them there."

"I guess they are," said Christopher, "but I never heard of anyone measuring things in perches." But Strike Three had a question for Plutonius that seemed to him far more important.

"What's time?" he asked.

The question surprised the children, but the reply surprised them even more for Plutonius said, "It is a measurement of something, that you cannot understand. It is a dimension into which you cannot enter."

"Surely anybody can understand time," said Christopher. "Minutes and days and months and years and so on. It's simple."

"No," said Plutonius. "Lumens cannot understand

time. They are immortal. Immortal means that there is no ending. If you are a creature for whom there is no ending to its existence, then you cannot understand what an ending is. And time depends for its very existence on a beginning and an ending, because it is a measurement. But it is a measurement outside of the scope of immortality. It is another dimension, and immortals cannot understand it."

"But I am a mortal and I can understand immortality," said Christopher. "I can understand things going on and on and on and not ending. I don't really mean that I can understand it," he added, "but I can accept that it is so."

"That is because you are human," said Plutonius, "and though in your present form you are mortal, you are in essence immortal and can glimpse both dimensions. You can also glimpse other dimensions which you do not understand or trouble your mind with and yet you are aware of them. That is what makes you humans the most fearful creatures in all space, so that even on Venus many tremble at the word 'human' and wonder what you are going to do."

"Why should they be afraid of us?" asked Christopher.

"Because of the power that lies in your hands," said Plutonius.

"What power?" asked Christopher, wondering if the lumens were referring to nuclear energy.

"A power we have not got, which you call thinking," said Plutonius. "We lumens do not understand it."

"But don't you think?" asked Christopher.

"No," said Plutonius. "We don't do what you call thinking. We know. There is a great difference. I feel, however, that we are soon to start thinking, and that disturbs me greatly."

While this conversation was going on, Arabella had gone with Patricia and Ita and Una to a beautiful expanse of flowers that looked very much like the anemones of Earth. They were of all colors and, to their delight, grew out of a bed of pink pearls. They made necklaces of the flowers and, when they were leaving, heard giggling and chattering behind them. They turned around and were astonished to see the flowers all talking one with the other. Then a little cloud of them rose up from the bed of pearls, like a flight of butterflies, and dividing into two, each group made of themselves a crown of beautiful colors and settled on the girls' heads.

"If you like us that much, we'll stay with you," said one flower.

"We can tell you lots of things," said another. "For instance, the surgeon fish found a creature that made a terrible noise and tried to swallow them. It is a sick creature, and soon all of us will be very sick because of it."

"There are swallowing monsters in the Seesuch now," said another. "One of them swallowed a piece of the Fruit of Journeys."

"And they were swallowing pieces of the Cliffs of Colors," said another.

"They'll swallow everything," said another, with a sigh, and then, brightening, added, "Maybe it's nice to be swallowed."

"Don't be such sillies," said Una. "The swallowing monsters you are talking about are these human children. This one is Patricia, and this one is Arabella, and they have two brothers, Kevin and Christopher, over there."

"Well, we only know what we're told," said one of the flowers, a little primly.

"You're little sillies, because you believe everything you hear," said Una.

"It's more fun that way," said the flowers, and giggled like children in a kindergarten.

"Don't pay any attention to the flowers," said Una. "They're just gossips, but they don't mean to make trouble."

"It's nice of them to make crowns for us," said Arabella. "And I like to hear gossipy things."

The flowers, with this encouragement, started to repeat all kinds of tidbits immediately. They said that one of the mermaids claimed that she had lost her mirror, but she had really given it to a centaur who lived on the top of the cliff that was above the Seesuch. She was tired of singing songs of ancient Greece and had fallen in love with the centaur and planned to run away with him, and they would live on the top of Mount Spera. At least, that was what the centaur said, but everybody knew that the centaur only wanted to capture the mermaid so that

she would bring him golden weed from the sea, which he liked to eat but could not get because he was forbidden to enter the Seesuch.

"And every bit of what I say is true," concluded the flower, "because Clione told me."

"Clione," said Una. "Why that little scatterbrain. She never gets anything straight."

"Who is Clione?" asked Patricia.

"The sea butterfly," said Una. "She floats around on the surface all day, coming down to the sea flowers when she wants to eat, for they give her nectar and in return she gives them gossip. She sees lots of things, but she hardly ever gets anything right. It is true that one of the mermaids has lost her mirror, but nobody knows where it is. It is just lost."

"Can't she get another?" asked Arabella.

"No. There are no others. Only the mermaids are allowed to have them. Nobody else on Nede is allowed to have a mirror or even look into a mirror," said Una.

"Why is that?" asked Patricia.

"I don't know," said Una. "Not even Plutonius knows."

By this time they were back with the others, and Arabella and Patricia had rejoined Kevin and Christopher, and Arabella said she still would like to see the nest of baby gorgons and there was plenty of time and they could swim there in a hurry.

"We can swim really fast," she said. "As fast as a seal or an eel or a creel."

"What's a creel?" asked Christopher.

"I don't know and I don't care," said Arabella. "Whatever it is, I can swim as fast as it. And I want to see the baby gorgons."

"Very well," said Plutonius. "But their nest is a long way away and you will have to ride. You can have a choice of a sea horse, a sea elephant, or a dolphin."

"Sea horse for me," cried Kevin and Arabella.

"I fall off horses," said Patricia. "An elephant sounds bigger and safer."

"I'll have a dolphin," said Christopher.

As soon as each had expressed his wish, the mounts appeared. A herd of sea horses came thundering in, snorting and tossing their magnificent manes, which flashed like surf breaking on a beach. The hindquarters were those of a fish, and the remainder of the beast was that of a horse, but half as big again as the horses of Earth. Some were bright blue, others red, others black, others white. Some were striped in black and gold like zebras and some were dappled in silver and black, and all were remarkably spirited and handsome.

Kevin seized the mane of a beautiful black horse and leaped on his broad back, and the horse reared up and whinnied and pranced in delight at having a rider. Arabella looked them over a little more carefully, and since she hesitated, they crowded around her, rolling their heads and eyes and making the bravest display with their manes in the hope of being selected.

"Do you want a smaller one?" asked Plutonius.

"No," said Arabella. "I'm looking for one bigger than Kevin's."

"Well, Kevin has the king of the herd," said Plutonius. "But I will call Bucephalus for you." Immediately a magnificent sea horse, black and white, with a lovely head white as snow but with a jet-black blaze down the broad forehead, appeared.

"Hooray," cried Arabella, and jumped on his back, and Ita placed herself just above the blaze like a tiny star.

Big as the horses were, the sea elephants were even bigger. They were not fat, shapeless, tusked creatures like the sea elephants of earth, but like real African elephants, strong and quiet and wise. The greatest number were dove gray, but some were black and some were pink. They were magnificently ornamented, with huge rings of gold about their legs, and their tusks studded with diamonds, and medallions of gold and rubies and emeralds hung upon their enormous foreheads. They had howdahs, or chairs, on their backs that looked like thrones, and beneath these, cloths were laid of lovely fabrics that had the sheen of satin and the allure of silk.

These sea elephants formed a huge circle around Patricia and, kneeling on their front legs, bowed before her, their trunks raised in dignified greeting. Patricia did not know which to choose, until she saw one whose medallion upon its forehead was formed of green stones in, it seemed, the shape of a shamrock.

"I'll take the Irish sea elephant," she said, her father being Irish.

"You've a face as fair as the first morning of the world," said the elephant. "Hop on me back and I'll make kindling of the rest of them." He extended his trunk, which he formed into a step. Patricia put her foot on it and was whisked with a certain flourish up on the elephant's back and placed with greatest ceremony in the golden howdah.

"It was Cuchulainn himself that rode there before you," said the elephant.

"I didn't know that he ever was on an elephant," said Patricia.

"Don't put anything past the Irish," said the elephant. "They'll surprise you every time."

The dolphins were, in their way, even more spectacular than the sea horses or sea elephants. They flashed by so fast that they were seen only as a shadow and then returned in a display of turquoise and silver, red, blue, and green that was beyond anything the children had seen so far. It seemed that they loved movement and stopped only after Plutonius had commanded them three times to be still.

The whites of their eyes flashed like diamonds, and the pupils gleamed like amethysts. Their bodies were covered with large scales that rippling with the slightest movement gave off tinkling notes and changed color at the same time, like shot silk. They were as large as the sea horses but had no mane and except for the scales were the same shape as porpoises on Earth. Each had a large fin on its back that was of frosted silver, and their mouths, or beaks, were a golden color.

"You chose well," said Plutonius. "The dolphins are the fastest creatures in the sea. But pick one quickly, for they hate to be still."

Christopher without hesitation jumped on the back of a dolphin who at that moment was all pink and green. He turned, in triumph, silver and red, and all then being mounted, they set off to find the nest of baby gorgons for Arabella and Patricia.

✳ · ✳ · ✳ · ✳ · ✳ · ✳ · ✳ · ✳

CHAPTER FOURTEEN

So swift were the children's mounts that the twenty-mile journey to the nest of the baby gorgons took less than an hour. The sea horses were exhilarating to ride. They propelled themselves forward with powerful sweeps of their gleaming tails, soaring upward in a splendid arc, their magnificent manes flowing behind them, so as to wrap, like a warrior's cloak, around Kevin and Arabella. At the end of these tremendous flights, the sea horses descended toward the bottom of the Seesuch, but only for a second. They thrust themselves off in an instant with their powerful forelegs, and then another sweep of the tail would send them soaring through the lovely blue of the sea in another graceful arc. Silver bubbles streamed from them as they soared along, and they shook their handsome heads with vigor and neighed and called to each other with voices as loud and triumphant as trumpets.

Compared with the sea horses, Patricia's Irish sea elephant lacked vigor and dash. But he made up for this with an imperial stride, stiff-legged and powerful and of enormous dignity, the heavy gold rings on his legs clashing, to announce his coming, like huge cymbals. His progress was all pomp and power, and even his somewhat ridiculously small tail (a member about which all elephants are sensitive) he curled behind him like a queue on a well-tended peruke wig. Every now and then he would reach with his trunk for a little gift for Patricia, whom he had decided to call "My lady"—a branch of coral exquisite as lace and royal purple in color, a sea anemone as brazen as a sunflower and as big as a dish, or a handful (or trunkful perhaps) of black pearls, scooped up with an elegant gesture and poured as a tribute into her lap.

Patricia was so pleased that she blushed with pleasure and looked all the prettier, and thanked the sea elephant for being so kind. But he said, "My lady, it is I that need to be thanking you, for the greatest joy of an elephant is to carry a queen, as I do at this very moment."

"What is your name, dear elephant?" asked Patricia, leaning forward to stroke its ears, which were as big as a blacksmith's apron.

"My lady, I am a modest creature and would blush to tell you a name as insignificant as my own."

"Oh, please do tell me, dearest elephant," said Patricia. "It must be a perfectly splendid name. Is it," she added, her voice a little trembly, "Herman, by any chance?"

"Oh, nothing splendid like that," said the elephant. "I'm useless with the guitar, and only my mother thought much of my voice, though I was the only one in our family that could get within a half tone of the high note in the Derry Air, and then only if I thought of a sea mouse. It's a small, humble name of no stature at all."

"I promise I won't tell a soul," said Patricia. "Please, please tell me what it is."

"It's Victory," said the elephant.

"But that's a tremendous name," said Patricia. "A magnificent name, particularly for an elephant."

"And kind it is of you to say it," said Victory. "But there's a sea elephant from Cork here that's called Triumphant, and I think I'll have to stretch him one of these days, the way he has of coming by and trailing his coat at me."

"But I thought all the creatures here were happy and loved each other and never quarreled," said Patricia.

"If I ever got into a place the likes of that," said Victory, "I'd get out of it fast enough; for it's the greatest pleasure to be able to stand nose to nose with someone and dare him to make a move."

While this conversation was going on, Christopher was having the most exciting ride of all on his dolphin. No sooner was he astride the beautiful scaled creature than it zoomed from the bottom of the Seesuch to the surface, broke the water in a cascade of silver spray that thundered down around them, and soared upward in the entrancing air, performing a lovely arc in the sky, and then, clean as a knife, dived below the surface again. This performance was done at jet speed, which made Christopher a little nervous, and he called to the dolphin, "Slow down. Slow down," and held on to the silver dorsal fin very tightly with both his arms.

The dolphin, however, either did not hear him or did not understand him, for it made a series of these tremendous leaps from water to air to water and then sped, swift as an arrow, underwater, so that all the beautiful colors were merged and blurred because they sped by so fast. All this was indeed frightening at first. But after a little while, when Christopher discovered that no harm had come to him, he relaxed and then began to enjoy the speed, and called to the dolphin to go faster and leap higher, which the dolphin was delighted to do.

They were not alone in this spectacular display, for a host of other dolphins joined them, all keeping perfect time—leaping together, reaching the apex of their lovely aerial arch together, and plummeting back into the water together. They circled the sea horses and the elephants with ease, dived under their legs and over their backs (which rather annoyed the sea horses), but Victory, the elephant, took no notice. He strode powerfully along, too dignified (despite his claims to modesty) to be disturbed by such antics.

When the dolphin leaped into the air above the Seesuch, Christopher was able to look about at what lay above the water, for they had had only a glimpse of the actual land of Nede before the flying saucer came down. He saw, off to his left, a coastline of tremendous cliffs, which he judged must be five or six hundred feet high. They soared far, far above the leaping dolphin, and near the tops of the cliff were flocks of birds, fluttering about and no bigger than the tiniest scraps of white paper.

In places these cliffs, heavily ribbed, were golden, in places white, in places black, and in places scarlet. There were trees growing on the sides in some locations, and the roots of many of these trees dangled like cords down the steep cliff face. But wherever they managed to touch the cliff again, another tree sprang up from the root, so that the trees that grew near the bottom of the cliff were sons, or perhaps great-grandsons, of those which had taken root at the top and which (Christopher decided) must be much bigger and very much older.

The surface of the Seesuch at this place was covered with roaring waves, deep blue but clothed with surf which was silver and pale gold. The surf slipped from the tops of these waves with a thundering noise into the troughs, and there was nothing the dolphin liked better than to burst midway out of a wave that was perhaps fifty feet high, clear the top of another as if it were a hedge, and then plunge midway into the next giant wave beyond.

There was a very heavy wind blowing, which caused the surf at this place, but the sky above had only the smallest wisps of clouds, so high that Christopher could not look up at them without becoming giddy.

For some time, of course, he was too busy to look about, for it is no small thing to saddle a dolphin and be plunged from one enormous wave over another and into the middle of a third. He kept wincing and bracing himself, expecting a tremendous impact as the dolphin hurtled toward the glistening wall of water. But there never was an impact—only a delightful sensation halfway between tickling and the tiniest stinging, so that he got to enjoy it and began to look about him.

The vast cliffs fascinated him, and at the top of the dolphin's leaps he could also see, over to his right and far ahead, a small scarlet island, surrounded by white foam, which came nearer and nearer with each leap. As they got closer, he saw that the lower part of the island was scarlet but there was a fringe of blue around it. And above that was a mountain that was pink in parts and gold in others.

"Is that where we're going?" Christopher asked, this being the first question he had put to the dolphin, partly because, up to this point, he had been a bit out of breath.

"Going?" squeaked the dolphin, in the kind of voice one would expect of a mouse. "We're not going anywhere. We're just having fun."

"But we're supposed to be going where the baby gorgons are," said Christopher.

"Are you a human being?" asked the dolphin.

"Of course I'm a human being," said Christopher.

"Do me a favor," said the dolphin, accelerating. This time he leaped so high in the air that he went clean over the scarlet island with the pink and white top and landed beautifully in the water on the other side.

"Favor, like what?" asked Christopher, getting his cautious look.

"Just a little old favor that won't cost you a thing," said the dolphin. "Want to jump back over the island again?" he added.

"No," said Christopher. "What's the favor?"

"Tell the other humans that we dolphins are very dumb," he said.

"Why?" asked Christopher.

"Because if they find out we're smart they'll put us to work," said the dolphin.

"They won't put you to work on Nede," said Christopher.

"If they put us to work on your planet, they'll put us to work here," said the dolphin.

"I'll do what I can," said Christopher. "But please take me now to where the baby gorgons are."

To his surprise, the dolphin turned completely around, to head back where they had come from. It seemed that he had thought Christopher didn't want to go anywhere in particular but just wanted to join in the fun of zooming out of the water into the air and back again. Still, his speed was such that they had rejoined the others in a very short while. They were gathered around a pinnacle of white coral that rose above the bottom of the Seesuch for a distance of perhaps thirty feet.

"Let the steeds stay here, so as not to frighten the gorgons," said Plutonius. "The children can come to the top and see the babies."

"Whistle when you want me," said the dolphin, and was gone in a flash, without waiting for a reply. "You must excuse him," said Plutonius. "It is very tedious for the dolphins to be still even for a second."

They swam up to the top of the pinnacle and found that at the summit was a depression that seemed to have been made in the coral artificially. In this depression lay what looked like a huge golden ball of some kind of kelp or weed.

"They're inside and probably asleep," said Plutonius.

"Oh, do call them out," said Arabella.

"All right," said Plutonius, and made a twittering kind of sound, like a chaffinch. Nothing happened for a moment, and then the golden ball started to roll around in the depression a little, and then the movement got more violent, as if there was a scramble going on inside.

And then, out of a circular hole in the side, popped five little blue creatures shaped rather like dormice but covered with scales. They had pale pink ears and the most elegant silver whiskers, and one of them put out its tongue, which proved to be about twice as long as itself. This seemed to be a poor thing for the baby gorgon to do, for its tongue (which was also blue), hanging down the side of the coral pinnacle, overbalanced the gorgon, and it teetered for a moment and fell tumbling to the bottom.

"Oh, the poor little thing," cried Arabella and Patricia together, and sped down after it to catch it before it hit the bottom. Plutonius watched the two girls play with the tiny blue, scaled creatures, and it seemed to Kevin that he was very thoughtful.

CHAPTER FIFTEEN

THE children discovered that the baby gorgons had tiny pink wings of a shade that exactly matched their ears, and three toes on each foot, armed with long curved claws, and a very small tail that at its present state of growth was nothing more than a bump and a promise. Plutonius told them that when the tail was fully developed it was a very fine tail indeed and helped to balance the gorgons when eating. But until their tails grew, they fell on their heads every time they put out their elegant long tongues.

Arabella wanted to take one back to the flying saucer, but Plutonius pointed out that she would not know how to take care of it, and furthermore it was at a stage when it would grow very rapidly now and in a little while would be as big as a sheep. Fully grown, the gorgon would be much bigger than the flying saucer, much too big for a pet. So, having played with them and petted them, the children left the gorgons, for the water of the

Seesuch was becoming just a little darker and Plutonius had remembered that they must be back before dark.

On the return ride, directed by the lumens, the children collected many kinds of fruits from the sea for dinner—sea cucumbers, sea eggs, sea hares, and golden sea grapes. They found a lovely grove of sea pears which were pink and silver and grew from purple trees. All these fruits were remarkable in that as soon as one was plucked, another formed on the tree in its place in a matter of seconds. They also got bouquets of the sea flowers, chattering away like a flock of sparrows, and returned to the flying saucer laden with spoils.

All except Christopher. Plutonius whistled for his dolphin, which appeared in a flash and gave Christopher the same ride back as he had experienced out—leaping high out of the water and plunging, all vigor and joy, into the back of the blue and silver waves. Again Christopher had to remind the dolphin that they were bound for the flying saucer. And the dolphin replied in his curious little whistling voice that he was very glad indeed he was not a human being, as human beings always had to have an object in view, and never did things just for the pure fun of doing things.

"Please, please, tell the other humans that we dolphins are all very dumb," he begged, and with a powerful thrust of his tail soared out of the Seesuch and over the scarlet island with the pink and green mountain, making a high-pitched noise that sounded to Christopher like "Wheee."

The sun was now getting quite low, giving to the ocean first a darker shade of blue, then turning the wave tops to gold, and then streaking them with red. Strike Three, who had of course remained with Christopher, began to get quite excited. "Soon it will be dark," he said. "Hooray!" replied the dolphin. "Dark is the best time. When it is dark, everything in the Seesuch gives out its own light, in its own colors. It's just beautiful."

"Listen, dumb dolphin," said Christopher. "Uncle Bill said we have to be back at the flying saucer by the time it's dark."

"It's only getting dark on this side," said the dolphin. "On the other side, where the flying saucer is, it's still light."

"Goodness," cried Christopher. "Are we that far away?"

"Don't worry," said the dolphin. "We can stay here until it's quite dark and see everything, and then I can take four big leaps and put you back by the flying saucer while it is still daylight."

"No tricks," said Christopher. "You take me back there right now. I don't want to be in the Seesuch when it's dark."

"Why not?" asked the dolphin, leaping up into the air (it was twilight now) and doing a spin, then falling back into the sea. "It's the fun time after dark."

"Because of something the Impatient Wise One doesn't want us to know about yet," said the lumen.

"Something called what?" asked the dolphin, speeding toward the bottom, where the dusk was already gathering and the creatures of the Seesuch beginning to glow in a kaleidoscope of lights.

"I forget the name," said Strike Three. "Something I've never heard of."

"Fear," said Christopher.

"That's right," said Strike Three. "What fun to meet something we have never seen before. Has fear got legs and arms like you?"

"Is it a dolphin?" asked the dolphin.

"It hasn't any shape," said Christopher.

"Hasn't any shape?" they both said together, very surprised. "But everything has to have a shape. What do you mean, it hasn't got any shape?"

"It's a feeling," said Christopher. "A feeling hasn't got a shape," he said, thinking of what Uncle Bill had explained to the children.

But neither the lumen nor the dolphin could understand what a feeling was. "Look," said Christopher. "When you're bounding around and jumping up into the sky and diving into the seas—watch that rock," for the dolphin was headed for one which was in the dark water, giving off a volcano plume of green smoke. "When you're jumping around like that, you enjoy it, right?"

"Right," squeaked the dolphin.

"Well, enjoying is a feeling," said Christopher. "And it hasn't any shape, has it?"

"Certainly it has a shape," said the dolphin. "It has

the shape of water and air and speed all put together. I could make a picture of it. It has that shape."

"Oh, you *are* dumb," said Christopher. "Those are just the things that give you the feeling. They are not the feeling itself. *They* may have a shape, but the feeling hasn't any."

"Well, what is the shape of the thing that gives you the other feeling?" said the dolphin.

"I don't know," said Christopher. "It can be all kinds of things, really," he added. "Things that want to harm you."

But the dolphin could not understand what harm was, and Christopher got tired of trying to explain it to him. The more he explained, the more puzzling it became for the dolphin, so Christopher gave up. But by now it was quite dark and everything under the surface of the Seesuch had undergone a complete change.

There was no lovely blue water now, but only dark emptiness. And in this dark, soft as velvet, every creature appeared in its own colors and lights, the scarlet hiding rocks, the golden forests with their red fruits, the silver growths of sea figs, the purple and black sea hares, and the pale violet sea eggs covered with graceful spines. These, which during the day had merely reflected the light of the sun, underwent a lovely night change, emitting light of their own, and now creatures invisible in the day came into view—segmented sea worms, feathered like Sioux Indian chiefs and with a fringe of scarlet legs undulating down each side of their bodies.

And sea pens, like old-fashioned quill pens, standing up from the bottom like ostrich quills, and beautiful fernlike creatures, some purple, some silver and scarlet, which were invisible or drab during the daylight. At one place, Christopher heard a measured creaking and cracking, as of someone opening and closing a heavy door with a squeaky hinge but to an exact time. And then there came into view whole regiments of lobsters, fierce as guardsmen, keeping time with their horny legs as they marched across the floor of the Seesuch and banging their claws in unison over their heads like castanets.

It was all fascinating, and Strike Three kept saying that this was only the start. But Christopher had an uneasy feeling that somewhere out in the darkness, beyond this wonderful display, something was watching and waiting, something malevolent.

"Come on," he said to the dolphin. "Let's get back to the flying saucer, right now."

"Couldn't we stay just a little while and perhaps catch a glimpse of fear?" asked Strike Three.

"No," cried Christopher. "We must go right now. I mean it."

"Oh, all right," said the dolphin, and zoomed from the water into the air, where Christopher caught just a glimpse of the upper edge of the sun as it was about to disappear below the horizon. At the next jump, the sun was higher up, being only halfway down in the sea. At the next, it was quite clear of the sea, and the fourth jump, which brought them to the flying saucer, showed the sun with perhaps ten minutes to go before it set.

"Phew," said Christopher, getting off. "That was fast."

"Bye," squeaked the dolphin, who just couldn't be still and was gone in a moment. Christopher swam up to the hatch in the flying saucer and found the others already there, having arrived half an hour before him.

"Where the heck have you been?" asked Uncle Bill. "I told you to get back here before dark."

Christopher didn't want to get the dolphin into trouble, so he said he'd been enjoying himself and had forgotten these instructions. This statement threw Strike Three into confusion. He darted all around Christopher, rather like one of the surgeon fish, and then, quite desperate, exclaimed to Uncle Bill, "Is this fear? Is this the thing that you don't want us to know? Oh, I understand why now. His vibrations are no longer concentric. He will have to be reharmonized."

"What the devil do you know about fear?" demanded Uncle Bill.

"It has no shape," said Strike Three, "and it has disturbed his vibrations."

"What do you mean, it has disturbed his vibrations?"

"He knew that he had to come back here before dark. He kept telling the dolphin so. He said so over and over again. But now he says that he forgot. So, plainly, his vibrations are disturbed. Is that what fear does? Oh, I don't like it at all."

"No, you dumb lumen," said Uncle Bill. "That isn't

fear. It's almost the opposite—it's a thing called loyalty. It is a tool humans use to combat fear."

"I hope my vibrations never become eccentric like that," said Strike Three.

"Don't worry," replied Uncle Bill. "You are created so that you cannot lie. It's one of the many advantages of being immortal. Though there are disadvantages, too."

"Like what?" asked Kevin.

"Like, for immortals there is no achievement and no failure. There is only continuance. Now let's get our dinners, and tell me what happened to you all today."

Christopher had expected that he ought to take a shower, but this proved quite unnecessary. Not only was he quite dry despite spending a day in the Seesuch, but he was absolutely clean and his skin tingled pleasantly and had a fresh and pleasing scent like pine needles, only better. When he came to comb his hair, he discovered that it wasn't knotted as was usual after swimming, and the girls' hair, which was long, was as soft and lustrous as if they had just come from a hairdresser.

For dinner they had a salad of sea lettuce and sea cucumbers, followed by an excellent hot soup of sea cabbage and then the main dish, sea hare in a spicy sauce. This had been prepared by Uncle Bill, who, in keeping with his character, gave the dish a fine French name, *Cervelle de mer, garni avec des vers de mer Maître Guillaume.* Kevin, who was rather good at French, translated this as "Sea hare with Maestro Bill's sea-worm sauce."

It tasted scrumptious, until Patricia, asking for a third helping, found out about the sea worms, whereupon the taste fell off a bit, though this didn't bother Christopher and Kevin, who cleaned their plates thoroughly.

"All right," said Uncle Bill when the table had been cleared away and the dishes washed (for he insisted that all work be done before they settled down to the enjoyment of conversation). "What did you horrid children see in your journeys that I did not—for I obviously don't want to hear about things with which I am familiar."

The children looked at each other puzzled. "I think you know of everything we saw," said Patricia.

"Oh, no, he doesn't," said Arabella. "Remember? He's never seen the mermaids."

"Mermaids," cried Uncle Bill, quite excited. "Did you really get to see them?"

"Yes, indeed," said Patricia. "And they sang a song for us."

"Never mind the song," snapped Uncle Bill. "I never could abide singing—particularly women. What did they tell you?"

"Tell us?" said Patricia. "They didn't tell us anything, I don't think. Except one told us her name—only she put it in a riddle. Uncle Bill, what star is the rival of Mars?"

"Oh, who cares," said Uncle Bill impatiently. "Didn't they tell you anything at all?"

"Only about Ancient Greece."

"What about Ancient Greece?"

"Something about a girl called Per . . . Per something."

"What happened to her?"

"She was taken down into a place under the earth and kept prisoner there but could return to the surface for six months out of each year," said Patricia. "It was very sad, but beautiful too."

"Persephone," said Uncle Bill. "Did they say anything else?"

"No," said Patricia. "They thanked us for the present we gave them and told that riddle about the stars when we wanted to know the name of the chief mermaid."

"Well, there's that stuff about the mirror," said Arabella.

"Oh, that was only the flowers gossiping," said Patricia.

"What stuff about the mirror?" asked Uncle Bill. "You talked to the flowers?"

"Yes. They left us just before we got here. They were blue and red and white, and some were smaller and were pink."

"Drat the colors," said Uncle Bill. "I am perfectly aware of the fact that flowers have different colors. Plutonius, did these children really talk to the flowers and the mermaids?"

"Yes, Impatient Wise One," said the Lumen.

"Tell me about the mirror." And the children told him how one of the mermaids had lost her mirror and it was rumored that she had given it to one of the centaurs. Uncle Bill thought about this for a long time and then said, "Well, there may have been a reason for you children making this trip after all. I have been unable even to see the mermaids, and the flowers have never spoken to me. But from what I have heard while you were away, coupled with the disappearance of the mermaid's mirror, I believe that Ka, the Smiler, has left Venus and is here on Nede now. You children may yet have a hand in saving Nede and the lumens from him."

CHAPTER SIXTEEN

It was Kevin who broke the silence that followed Uncle Bill's surprising pronouncement. He was, because of his dream of Ka, the Smiler, more aware than the others that there was something wrong in Nede, that some formless but definite threat hung over the beautiful and happy place.

"You'd better speak plainly to us, Uncle Bill," he said. "You really haven't told us much about Nede at all. If there is a threat of danger, then we ought all to know of it." But Uncle Bill made no immediate reply to this. He appeared to be in deep thought, as if he had not heard Kevin speaking, so Kevin said, "Uncle Bill, did you land the flying saucer in the Seesuch because, as you say, nobody can come to any harm here? If we had come down on the land, would we have been in danger?"

"There's nothing to be frightened of," said Uncle Bill, glancing at Arabella, who looked a little nervous. "It isn't a matter of danger at all, as you understand it. Nothing that can hurt you, or anything like that. . . .

It's, er . . ." He did not finish the statement, and Plutonius said, "Now the Impatient Wise One's vibrations are not concentric. Tell me, is this the thing called fear you told us of, or is it the thing called loyalty?"

"It's neither," said Uncle Bill with a grin. "It's a thing called dissimulation, which is a lie dressed up in its Sunday clothes and pretending to sing in a choir. Oh, well. No sense in doing anything but sticking to the plain truth, with these lumens around." But Plutonius was interested in lies, which he could perceive as eccentric vibrations in the brain.

"Can you produce these vibrations when you want?" he asked.

"Yes," said Uncle Bill.

"How strange," said Plutonius. "We can do nothing of the sort. In fact, the very concept of doing so is almost beyond our grasp. Have you humans always been able to do this?"

"As far as we know," said Uncle Bill.

"You don't know when it was first done?" asked Plutonius. "Surely there would be a record or a memory of a change as important as that."

Uncle Bill hesitated, but it was Patricia who supplied the answer. "There was a tree," she said. "It grew in a beautiful garden called Eden, and we were not supposed to eat any of the fruit. There were only two of us then, Adam and Eve. But Eve ate the fruit, and then Adam did, and afterward they lied about it, and that was the first lie told. Everybody knows of that," she added. "It was the most important thing that ever happened to us."

"What was the name of the tree?" asked Plutonius.

"It was called the Tree of the Forbidden Fruit," said Patricia.

"Its real name," said Uncle Bill solemnly, "was the Tree of Knowledge of Good and Evil. Whoever ate its fruit could distinguish good from evil and could choose between the two freely."

"Good and evil," said Plutonius, puzzled. "Oh, you humans. How very confusing you are, and how different from us. You talk of things that we have never heard of. What is good and what is evil?"

The children looked at each other, dismayed at being asked to define such a huge concept. The lumens had gathered in a circle on the table, with Plutonius in the center. Whenever they had a problem, they seemed to nudge together, as if in so doing, each reinforced the other in their efforts to cope with it.

Uncle Bill looked at them thoughtfully and said, "It is time you learned of this, so pay the closest attention. Nede didn't just happen, nor Venus, nor Earth, nor the Sun. They were all created as part of a Plan, as was the whole universe. In short, there is a Plan for everything in our universe and every creature in the universe."

"We know that," said Plutonius. "That is very evident to us."

"All right," said Uncle Bill. "This is where it gets complicated. If there is a Plan, there must be a Planner, someone who drew up the Plan." The lumens moved a little closer to each other at this statement, indicating that the going was indeed getting a little hard for them.

"A Planner?" said Strike Three. "A One Thing all alone? Oh, that disturbs my vibrations. Oh, please tell us nothing more until they settle down."

Uncle Bill waited. The light of the lumens had dwindled and flickered until it was only a blue glow, but then it came back steadier and it seemed to the children a little stronger. The light of Plutonius, however, had not even flickered, indicating that he had learned nothing new. When the lumens had recovered, Uncle Bill said, "Better move in closer to each other, lumens, for you will need each other's help when you hear what has to follow.

"You asked what is good and what is evil. Good is whatever is thought or done that promotes the Plan of the Planner. Evil is whatever is thought or done that interferes with the Plan of the Planner."

The effect on the lumens of this quite simple statement was startling. Their light dwindled to a ring of tiny blue buds, like those on a stove when the gas has been turned off. And then they went out with a kind of a pop. But a moment later they were back again, appearing one here and one there, and of an orangey color.

"Oh, poor things," said Arabella. "You've made them all sick."

"They'll be all right," said Uncle Bill. "But I wish I

didn't have to do this. It's very hard on them. And yet I think it is time."

"It is time, indeed," said Plutonius. "It is time for the leap. I have always known we had to make one. That is why I found you on Earth and brought you here. You must help us to make the leap."

Gradually but firmly the light of the lumens returned. It wasn't, however, quite as blue now. There was still a blue tinge, but more subdued, and as a consequence the light was brighter.

"You have started on the leap," said Uncle Bill, noting this. "Now you cannot turn back until it is finished. So have courage, and I will continue."

"Courage means stand together," said Strike Three, and they moved again closer to each other.

"If there is a Planner with a Plan," said Uncle Bill slowly, "it is possible, indeed probable, that there is an Anti-Planner with an Anti-Plan."

That did it. The lights of the lumens went out without even a pop, and even that of Plutonius dwindled until it was no bigger than a tiny blue bead from a doll's necklace.

"Oh, you've killed them all," cried Arabella. "Ita! Ita! Please come back." And Patricia said, "Una! Dear Una! Please come back." Even Christopher, who was at an age when he felt himself above sentiment, said, "Hey. Strike Three. Come on, Strike Three. Please don't go away." And then, to Uncle Bill's surprise, the three lumens reappeared painfully slowly, so that first of all there was just a ghost of a glow on the table, which turned into a reflection of light and after a while became light itself. In the same manner, the other lumens came back, but much more slowly, and only Plutonius, who had been the biggest of them all, remained tiny and fragile in the center of the ring of lights.

"Plutonius," cried Kevin. "What's the matter? Can I help you?" He turned to Uncle Bill. "What can I do for him?" he asked. "We must help him." But these words were hardly said before Plutonius's light grew bigger and stronger, and very rapidly indeed, until once again it was steady and bright and, as before, bigger than that of the others.

"I have just learned something," said Uncle Bill, staring at this effect. "Plutonius, what strengthened you?"

"Kevin's voice," said Plutonius. "Everything was conflicting, and my energy was being used to diminish itself. Then Kevin called my name and the conflict ended, and now I know a great deal more."

"What did you learn, Uncle Bill?" asked Kevin.

"The power of concern," said Uncle Bill. "The power that comes from one creature caring for another, however different they may be. Plainly, it was the closeness of you children to the lumens that brought them back so rapidly, for I am sure that you observed that those whose names were called with anxiety were the first to recover. Very interesting. Affection as a measurable force in the destiny of creation. Hmmmmmm. And then some of our postgraduates grumble that they are incapable of finding an original topic for research for their doctorates. Highly polished and stultified intellects; excellent as marble and useless as minds."

"Whatever are you talking about, Uncle Bill?" asked Patricia.

"Modern education—what else?" asked Christopher.

"Uncle Bill," said Kevin, "we haven't gotten around to whatever is the matter with Nede. We've been talking about things that haven't anything to do with it."

" 'Gotten,' " said Uncle Bill. "Odd, isn't it, how that ancient Saxon ending, utterly lost in England, should survive in America? Have you ever thought why that should be?"

"Uncle Bill," said Kevin. "You're stalling."

"I'm not stalling at all," said Uncle Bill. "I'm just attempting to demonstrate the possibilities for learning that exist all around if you'll only develop your curiosity and ask yourselves some questions."

He looked about at the lumens, took out his curved stem pipe, lit it, and the lumens edged a little away from him, for they were not fond of tobacco, though they did not object to it strongly, because they had concluded that smoking was something the Impatient Wise One needed to steady his vibrations—in short, to help him think.

"Well, you seem to be in pretty good shape," he said. "So brace yourselves and we'll continue. You have, however distressing it is for you, got a concept at least of a Planner and a Plan, and an Anti-Planner and an Anti-Plan." The lumens flickered a little but were able to accept this now without being extinguished.

"All you creatures on Nede," said Uncle Bill, "have not had to be concerned with this in the past because you automatically followed the Plan, which you did not even know existed—just as Nede circling Venus and Venus circling the sun as does our planet Earth, each in its appointed cycle, follow the Plan without being conscious of doing so or thinking about it in any degree.

"We on Earth, however, have been actually aware of the Plan for thousands of years. I do not mean that we understood or we understand its details, or even understand its broad form, or its object. But we do know that the Plan is there and have known that it is there since shortly after the first of us was created. We were made aware of the Plan oddly, not by the Planner, but by the Anti-Planner. It was he who persuaded Eve to eat of the fruit of the Tree of Knowledge of Good and Evil. And once she and her partner Adam became aware of good and evil, they became aware of the Plan, for the key to discovering the existence of the Plan is to become aware that there is good and that there is evil.

"Once, then, we on Earth knew of the Plan, we had a choice of following it or opposing it and supporting the Anti-Plan."

"What did you do? What did you do?" cried the lumens in chorus. "Oh, we begin to know what fear is now. Tell us what you did, because we are afraid, we think."

"Fear is good when it warns and bad when it masters," said Uncle Bill. "You need fear now, and the Planner has seen that you got fear when you needed it. Though I am sorry to have been the one who brought it to Nede."

"We love you. We do not blame you," said the lumens. "But tell us what you humans did on earth. We are very afraid of your answer."

"Some of us chose the Plan and tried to work in accordance with it insofar as we could understand it. We had many interpretations of the Plan, but there were common factors in all of these interpretations, and our reason taught us that these common factors must really belong to the Plan, whatever might be thought of the differences. So some of us accepted these factors. But others followed the Anti-Plan because they thought that would bring them more contentment and happiness. They obeyed the common factors only when it profited them personally, irrespective of what hurt it did to others. Some denied that there was either a Plan or a Planner. They said everything just happened without any reason. Many of these still followed the Plan, though, but only for love of their fellows."

As the children had expected, the lights of the lumens went dimmer and dimmer during this explanation, and they moved closer and closer to each other to lend strength to their vibrations. Yet at the end the light was still there, and that of Plutonius remained greater than the rest.

"How could this be possible?" said Strike Three. "How could it be possible for human beings to do different things? Aren't they all humans alike, as all lumens are alike? How could one do one thing and one do another thing? How could that be?"

"Because, unlike you lumens, human beings are all individuals and can act by themselves and think by themselves," replied Uncle Bill. "You lumens think with a collective mind, or at least with a mind that is so uniformly formed that you all think the same. But humans are not so constructed, and each can think for himself."

"That must be terrible," said Strike Three. "To be by yourself. Oh, now the new frightening is worse than ever."

CHAPTER SEVENTEEN

UNCLE BILL's explanation of the reason for his present voyage to Nede took some hours. This was not because the mission itself was so involved but because the lumens had enormous difficulty in grasping some of the terms that he used which were quite beyond their experience or even their speculation. Terms such as "harm," "heal," "good," "evil," "courage," "loyalty," "betrayal," "faith," "hope," "hate," which the children could readily understand, made no sense to the lumens, with the exception at times of Plutonius, who had, now and again, a wisp of understanding of some of these actions and qualities.

He, their leader, was the most evolved of the lumens, and it was he who had first sensed a threat to the planet and the lumens and had come to the Impatient Wise One, as they called him, on Earth, for aid.

The lumens had visited Uncle Bill on Earth several times before he came to believe in their existence, discovered how to communicate with them, and then, having built the flying saucer out of fiberglass, visited their planet. After the first visit, he had been so delighted with himself that he had painted the picture that the children had seen at his house in Coppertown. He had shown himself in a space suit out of sheer exuberance, for no space suit was necessary on Nede or in the flying saucer traveling there. Still, as he pointed out, a knight is usually depicted in armor and a space traveler in a space suit. As for the mix-up over the children's arrival at Coppertown, Uncle Bill had completely forgotten they were coming.

"I was needed back here urgently," he said, "and so you had to come, for you had discovered the existence of the lumens too, and believed in them.

"And now I come to the critical point which everyone, lumens and children, must be told and must try to understand to the very best of their ability. You children will understand readily enough, I think. You lumens will just have to take much of what I say for granted and act on it as directed. Later—much, much later—you may understand it.

"You lumens are beginning to evolve—to change—and that is plainly part of the Plan. You are changing from group-conscious creatures, all thinking alike and acting alike, to individually conscious creatures such as human beings are. Like us, however, you will retain for a long time many of the group-conscious reactions of your inheritance.

"For the sake of the children, I will give you an

example of what I mean. We human beings, although able to think and act individually, still retain certain group reactions. For instance, if there is a sudden loud noise near a group of people, they all react the same way. They flinch and duck. If our nerves are overstimulated by fear or excitement, we all scream, though screaming does nothing to remove the cause of the overstimulation. And so on. As it is with us, so it will be with you lumens. The important thing is, though, that you are rapidly getting to the point where you can act on your own—where you can make an individual choice between one course of action and another.

"You must learn, then, to choose between good and evil, which are terms you can scarcely understand at present. The Anti-Planner will try to get you to choose what is evil, for he knows of your evolution. But if you do, Nede will no longer be a place of happiness. And you should all know by now who is the Anti Planner. He has a name. Each one of you tell me his name—Plutonius last of all."

It was almost painful to see the lumens try to answer a question as individuals—a question that called for reflection before an answer could be supplied. At first they refused to do so. They just clustered together and all together cried out whatever name came to them through their mutual vibrations. The replies were mere group reactions and quite ridiculous—they said the mermaids, the dolphins, the sea elephants, and even, to their horror, Uncle Bill. And when this was done, and they still clustered together, except Plutonius, who edged nearer to the group but still managed to remain separated, Uncle Bill pointed out patiently how futile these group reactions were.

"You are making any reply that is comforting to you all, irrespective of whether it is true or not," he said. "You are not thinking. You are looking for comfort and not for truth. You must by yourselves, individually, state what you believe to be true, whether it comforts you or not.

"Now you, Strike Three. Move aside from the others and answer me. Who do you think is the Anti-Planner?" Under this pressure, it was difficult enough to get Strike Three to move away from the others. When this was achieved and the question was put to him repeatedly, his light got dimmer and dimmer and dimmer until it nearly went out and Christopher begged Uncle Bill to stop asking the question. The lights of all the other lumens got dimmer as well, but not quite as dim.

This pleased Uncle Bill, though he had not got his answer. "I begin to see an individual reaction among the lumens for the first time," he said. "All their lights are dimming, but Strike Three's is dimming more than the others. He is reacting individually. That kind of reaction was unheard of when I first visited Nede."

"I think you are pushing them too hard," said Christopher. "Let them go on reacting together, as a group, for a while. It isn't doing them any harm."

"That is exactly what the Anti-Planner wants," said

Uncle Bill. "He would like to keep them in a group state, like a shoal of fish or a flock of birds, all darting in the same direction and at the same time and for no good reason. In that manner, he can control and rule them readily."

But efforts to get the other lumens to answer the question as individuals likewise failed. Uncle Bill didn't try with Ita because she was so tiny. And anyway Arabella said that he wasn't to ask his "stupid old question" of Ita, and when Uncle Bill wasn't looking, she coaxed Ita into a saucepan and put the lid on, so Uncle Bill wouldn't know where she was.

Una failed miserably to supply the answer, and so did several others of the lumens. It was hard enough even to get them to leave the crowd. But to answer, when alone, was impossible for them, though together they would cheerfully shout any answer at all.

"Well," said Uncle Bill, shrugging, "I shouldn't be discouraged. We humans, under pressure, react the same way. Faced with some kind of threat to our society, we get into a crowd for comfort and name as an enemy any one at all."

"Maybe they don't even know who the Anti-Planner is," said Kevin. "All this stuff is new to them. Plan and Anti-Plan, Planner and Anti-Planner. They're kind of innocent. They don't know anything."

"But they've *got* to know," said Uncle Bill. "Their safety lies in knowing. They *have* to find out and they *have* to demonstrate that they can act individually.

That's why I'm here. I can't stand guard over them. They have to guard themselves."

He turned then to Plutonius. "You," he said. "Can you answer the question? Who is the Anti-Planner?"

When the question was put to him, Plutonius reacted immediately by moving closer to the others. In fact, it seemed that he was going to join in the cluster of lumens, and the children watched him anxiously, hoping that he would not do so. But he moved so close to the other lumens that his own light merged on one side with theirs. And then, with a great effort it seemed, he moved away—not very far away but far enough so there was a distinct separation between him and the rest.

He remained in this position for some time and then, quite slowly, moved still farther away, which brought a cheer from Kevin, who said, "Good old Plutonius. He'll make it. I know."

"Impatient Wise One," said Plutonius. "I cannot answer you. I cannot answer you." He repeated the statement several times, in such a way that they knew it was because of fear that Plutonius could not answer, though whether fear of the Anti-Planner or fear of the exercise of his own powers of thought and of decision, they could not say. Fear in itself was so new an emotion for Plutonius that for a while he could not recognize it, and when he did he cried out almost with relief, "Oh. It is the new thing—fear. I did not understand what was happening to me." He seemed almost relieved when he recognized his reaction.

"Answer, then," said Uncle Bill. "Name the Anti-Planner." But the chief lumen's light began again to dim and flicker, though he did not move any closer to the others. They also began to flicker, reacting in a group and in unison with Plutonius as if they were a mere reflection of him.

"Uncle Bill," said Kevin. "You won't get an answer that way. Let me try."

"Do you think you are smarter than I am?" said Uncle Bill angrily.

"No," said Kevin. "I don't, Uncle Bill. I just think you're handling it wrong."

"Oh, I am, am I?" said Uncle Bill. "Well, let me tell you that I've taken my degree in zoology and biology and I think I know something about kinetic reaction among the lower vertebrates. But if you think I was just wasting my time taking these courses, and you know better, go ahead."

"It isn't that, Uncle Bill," said Kevin. "I just want to try. But of course if you are afraid to have me try, I won't."

"Afraid to have you try?" roared Uncle Bill. "I'm not afraid of the great bronze bull of Bashan, or wherever they had bronze bulls. Go ahead and try until you're blue in the face and drop dead of frustration. See if I'm afraid to have you try."

"Okay," said Kevin and turned to Plutonius.

"Plutonius. You know of the Plan?"

"Yes."

"And the Anti-Plan?"

"Yes."

"And the Anti-Planner?"

"Yes." But before making that reply Plutonius paused and his light flickered.

"We want to know the name of the Anti-Planner," said Kevin. "Is it me?"

"No."

"Is it Christopher?"

"No."

"Is it Arabella?"

"No."

"Is it Ita?"

"No—but Ita must get out of the Impatient Wise One's saucepan or she will make it radioactive."

"Come on out then," said Arabella, removing the lid, and tiny Ita popped out and made a beeline for the other lumens because she needed comforting.

"It is none of those names?" continued Kevin.

"No."

"But the Anti-Planner must have a name?"

"Yes."

"So is it Ka, the Smiler?"

Plutonius's light flickered out like a candle in a gust of wind. But it returned immediately, and he cried, "Yes. Ka, the Smiler. He is the one. He is the Anti-Planner. It is he. It is he."

And immediately all the other lumens cried out in unison, "Ka, the Smiler, is the Anti-Planner. Ka, the

Smiler, is the one." They then formed a circle with Plutonius as center and whirled around him, crying, "Ka, the Smiler. Ka, the Smiler." And they made a crown around Kevin's head, with Plutonius, whose light was now even bigger than ever, like an especially large jewel in the front.

"Fine thing," said Uncle Bill grumpily. "Spend my time studying biology and zoology and this kid turns out to be smarter."

"I'm not smarter than you, Uncle Bill," said Kevin. "It's just that you've always lived alone, I guess, and so you don't know how to deal with kids. And these lumens are a lot like kids. If you give them a choice of answers, they can pick out the right one. But they don't like to be conspicuous. They feel shy or something when they are made to stand by themselves and answer a question."

"What's shy?" asked Strike Three.

"I can't tell you exactly," said Kevin. "But it's what you feel when you are standing alone and everyone is staring at you."

"Oh," cried the lumens in unison, and all together their lights went out. They came back a second later and in chorus begged Kevin not to spring a description like that on them again. "Please do it in little pieces," they said. "We get out of harmony when it is done all at once." Kevin promised to be more careful in the future.

It was almost midnight by Nede time before the children got to bed that night. By then Uncle Bill had explained that Ka, the Smiler, who lived on Venus, was almost certainly now on Nede. He would be on the land, for he could not enter the Seesuch, which would permit only good below its waters. He believed that the disappearance of the mermaid's mirror was the work of Ka, and while they had been exploring the Seesuch, he had questioned the creatures on the land, who had said that Ka had come from Venus with his emerald bowl.

"We must find him," said Uncle Bill, "and we must drive him back to Venus."

"Why do we have to drive him out?" asked Strike Three.

"Because he is the Anti-Planner," said Plutonius.

"What is happening to me that I did not know that? I knew it before," said Strike Three.

"What is happening is that you are becoming an individual and relying on an individual rather than a collective memory," said Uncle Bill. "Your individual memory is not very strong now, but it will grow."

"Is that what you call good?" asked Strike Three.

"It is part of the Plan and therefore it must be good," said Uncle Bill.

"Now that you have brought us fear, do not desert us, Impatient Wise One," said the lumens, and they collected in his lap for comfort.

CHAPTER EIGHTEEN

THE following morning Uncle Bill, the lumens, and the children went ashore on Nede. Despite the grave talk that Uncle Bill had had with the lumens the night before about the Anti-Planner, Ka, the Smiler, they were neither solemn nor preoccupied but as joyful as if they were going on a picnic. Certainly they did not show any concern over the threat of Ka or over the task that lay ahead of them, of forcing him to return to Venus. In fact, they annoyed Uncle Bill by forming one of their rings and whirling around the flying saucer out of sheer high spirits at the thought of going on the land and showing the children all the wonders there.

Even Kevin, who had become a kind of defender of the lumens, thought they ought to quiet down a bit and was concerned at their lack of gravity. But Christopher, after thinking about it, announced that the lumens had a good collective memory but a very weak individual memory and had then, individually, forgotten about Ka.

"They haven't known about being individuals for

twenty-four hours yet," he said. "In any case, they are only just born."

Arabella, after a night's sleep, didn't give a fig for Ka and wished aloud that she could whirl around the flying saucer with the lumens, because it seemed to be such fun.

"Certainly you can," said Plutonius. "Touch Ita and Una, one with each hand, and around you'll go." Arabella did so and in a moment was flying around the space ship, screaming both out of fright and out of excitement, her pale gold hair trailing behind her.

This of course looked like too much fun to be missed, so Patricia joined in, and then Christopher and Kevin, each arranging himself in the circle in such a way as to have a lumen touching either hand. Then round and round they went, doing somersaults and rolls and back flips, with legs and arms flying (though the lumens were careful to stay one on each hand), while Uncle Bill got madder than hops and demanded to know if this was any way to set out on a serious expedition to find and rebuff the malignant Ka.

But his shouted protests did him no good. The lumens after a while became conscious of him outside the saucer, shaking his fists at them, and the circle of lumens and children swooped down, and before he knew it, Uncle Bill was whirling around the flying saucer too, the circle going faster and faster, changing its axis occasionally and even once or twice reversing itself, which brought shrieks from all. When at last the lumens had

had enough and everybody settled down to the bottom of the Seesuch, Plutonius said soberly to Uncle Bill, "What you said about humans is true indeed. They have remnants of collective consciousness. For when we reversed the circle you all shrieked together."

This display of individual thought by Plutonius so pleased Uncle Bill that he forgot about being angry. And he was even more pleased when he found that Plutonius, by himself, without using a collective mind, had invited the children to join the demonstration.

They decided to leave the flying saucer in the Seesuch, and when they needed to travel fast, or a long distance, over the land, to use the lumens, one on each hand. The children remembered that in the picture he had painted of himself Uncle Bill had lumens in each hand. "That is how I travel about Nede and between Nede and Venus," said Uncle Bill. "Those are short distances. But between Earth and Nede I need the saucer, not because of cosmic radiation or other nonsense out of the comics, but because it's nice to have chairs around and bookshelves and a bed to lie in."

"Have you really been to Venus, too?" asked Kevin.

"Certainly I have," said Uncle Bill.

"With those terrible rainstorms and that red sky, it must be an awful place," said Kevin.

" 'All is in the eye of the beholder,' " quoted Uncle Bill. "If you make up your mind to like red skies and thundering rain, there's no nicer place in the universe than Venus." But at this the lumens twinkled with laughter and Uncle Bill himself grinned. "Well," he said, "it isn't a place to take children."

Everything being now ready, they swam up from the bottom of the Seesuch to the surface, where, to their surprise, they found breathing a little more difficult than in the water. They had to breathe faster to get the same amount of benefit, and found the air did not taste as good as in the Seesuch. And yet, after a little while, they found the surface air more exciting than that which they extracted from the water, for it brought to them strange scents, some heavy with perfume, some spiced, some harsh as if containing wood smoke, and some sappy as if succulent vines had been crushed nearby. They realized that there were no scents at all in the Seesuch, and their sense of smell, unused for a little while, now seemed very keen and a source of immense pleasure to them.

The surface was quite rough and frightening. Steep waves ran strangely out from the shore and crested over their heads. It seemed quite useless to swim against these, and the sensible thing, so Kevin thought, would be to go below the surface and swim submerged to the land. But, to his surprise, he found himself taken by some strong current, with his sisters and brother, toward the shore against the waves. In a few minutes he could touch bottom, and they all landed in shallow water ridged by the tiniest ripples, or baby waves, all running out to sea and getting bigger and bigger as they went.

"That's the morning wind of Nede," said Uncle Bill.

"Do you see the mountain there called Matalin?" The mountain peak showed deep blue against the sky and was ribbed in white. "In the morning, cold air, which is heavy, rolls down that mountain, displacing the warmer air below and causing a wind which blows offshore. When the sun is higher, the air on the mountaintop and slopes is warmed and the wind drops and then reverses itself in the afternoon, so that the wind then is off the Seesuch and onto the land. Well, let's climb the cliff and be on our way."

"Do you know of a particular place we are heading toward?" asked Kevin.

"Certainly I do," said Uncle Bill. "I'm going first to the Valley of the Centaurs beyond the cliffs. Drat it," he exclaimed. "I knew I had forgotten something."

"What?" asked Kevin.

"Some of the golden weed. It's useless to ask the centaurs to help without bringing them a gift."

So back they went into the Seesuch and collected armfuls of golden weed. This, though not particularly heavy, for it was full of little beads containing not vegetable pulp but air, was bulky. So they flew to the clifftops with the aid of the lumens, each carrying a bundle of the golden weed. When they got there, they found first an area going back from the cliffs for perhaps fifty yards which was covered with sharp glistening white stones, like flint. This lay all the way along the top of the cliff, as if it were a roughly made roadway.

"It's the exercise track of the centaurs," said Uncle

Bill. "They made it themselves, and it runs for twenty miles along the cliffs and back, in a circle. They gallop along it twice a day, in the morning and in the evening." He stopped for a minute, listening, and then said, "Hurry to the other side. They're coming now."

They had hardly got across the track before in the distance they saw a silver dust cloud that grew bigger and bigger with the passing of each second. Then they heard a slight drumming that grew louder and louder until it was like heavy gunfire or thunder, and the ground around them shook. On whirled the dust cloud, with nothing to be seen in it, and louder became the drumming of hundreds of hooves. And then they caught sight of magnificent horse heads all white and with golden manes, tossing in the cloud of stone dust. In a flash, the herd of centaurs had gone by, creating such a wind that it plucked at the children's clothes and hair and covered them with dust, and they were caught in a hail of flying stones. The drumming of the horses diminished, and when the children could see again, the dust raised by the centaurs was only a small puff far away down the track.

"Nasty things," said Arabella, brushing herself off. "They could have hurt us."

"Boy, they were really traveling," said Kevin.

"I thought centaurs had heads like human beings," said Christopher.

"That is a myth handed down from the Greeks," said Uncle Bill. "The Greeks tried to make everything human, even their gods. Centaurs are actually horses with wings."

"Wings?" cried Patricia. "I didn't see any wings."

"Well, they have them. But they don't use them when galloping. Only when they have to jump," said Uncle Bill. "Now, they'll come back soon, for although they went by so fast, their eyesight is enormously keen and they will have seen us, and seen the golden weed, so they'll return. And everybody be very polite, for centaurs are extraordinarily touchy. Vain, stupid, and pigheaded, in my opinion. Vulgar, in fact, as you will soon see when you talk to them. You won't find an aitch in a herd of them. But useful, for, of all creatures, they travel most and see most."

The centaurs returned at the same earth-shaking gallop a few minutes later and pulled up, milling around the children, showering them with small stones and dust and clods of earth, which was very uncomfortable and a little frightening. Even when they stopped galloping, they couldn't stop moving, but reared up and trotted toward the children and sidled away and curvetted about them and snuffled and snorted and made darts toward the golden weed.

One of them even bared his large teeth and nipped some of the golden weed from the bundle Patricia was carrying, and finding this was not resisted (for Patricia was nervous) came back for more. This, however, was more than Patricia was prepared to tolerate, so she slapped the centaur on his velvet muzzle, and immediately they all stood stock-still and stared first at the centaur who had been slapped and then at Patricia.

"First-class," said Uncle Bill sarcastically. "How to make friends and influence people. When you meet a stranger, slap him on the nose."

"Well, he frightened me and kept stealing my weed," said Patricia. "And I'm not going to be pushed around by any old centaur."

"Wot d'yer mean, 'any old centaur,' " said the one who had been slapped, speaking in an accent that Patricia recognized immediately and with delight.

"Oh," she cried. "Are you from Liverpool? Do you know Herman and his Hermits?"

"Me name's 'erman," said the Centaur. "Wot d'yer mean by slapping a bloke on the snapper?"

The other centaurs came immediately to his support, saying variously: "Proper battle-ax, ain't she?"

"Not what you could call a lidy."

"Ups with 'er duke and pops a bloke right on the beak."

"Din't even siy, 'Good morning, kiss me 'and,' or 'Bob's yer uncle.' Just whap—right on poor old 'erman's schnozzle."

"Blood in 'er eye—'at's wot she's got—blood in 'er blooming optic."

"Oh, phooey," said Arabella. "Your stupid old Herman stole some golden weed and deserved to be slapped."

"Now, now," said Uncle Bill. "That's no way to talk to the centaurs."

"Wot's that you got on yer chin—somebody's 'air cut?" said another, turning on him immediately.

"Got 'is 'ead on upside down—'at's wot's the matter wiv 'im," said a third.

"You leave Uncle Bill alone," said Arabella, and the centaurs immediately turned their attention to her, crying, "Watch out for tich." "Get your snozzle out of the way, 'erman," and so forth.

This situation might have gone on to no definite conclusion had not Kevin interfered. He took a handful of golden weed and holding it out said, "You guys like to try some of this? We got it for you specially."

"Now yer talking," said one of the centaurs and snapped up the golden weed in an instant. "Got 'is 'ead screwed on all right, that one," said another, and so they continued, complimenting first Kevin and by degrees, as they were offered and accepted golden weed, Christopher, then Arabella, and even Patricia. But though they ate all of Uncle Bill's golden weed, they wouldn't say what could be called a good word for him. They made ribald jokes at his expense and remarks about his bald head and his beard, which were a little hard to bear, and whereas the lumens called him the Impatient Wise One, the centaurs (with reference to his bald head) called him Shiny.

There seemed to be no leader among the centaurs. For all their physical strength and grace, they were a rowdy, rough democratic mob, given to jokes that were just a little coarse, and fond of making personal remarks. Herman, it turned out, was the one who had coaxed the mermaid into parting with her mirror, and they all knew of his plot to get her to bring the golden weed to him under the pretense of romance.

"Proper lad, is 'erman," said one, and they all winked in quite a vulgar way, and Arabella said they should give the mirror back immediately because it wasn't fair to take it from the mermaid.

"Any time, tich, any time," said Herman, cantered off, and returned with the mirror, which he gave to Arabella. She immediately put the mirror on the ground and knelt down to fix her hair, and Patricia, leaning over her shoulder, did the same.

Uncle Bill now asked the centaurs whether in galloping about the land they had noticed anything unusual, but before they would answer, he had first to promise to give them more golden weed. Having promised this, he then, to his annoyance, had to get it right away because, as the centaurs put it, a little golden weed in the mouth is better than a ton in the Seesuch.

Not to be trusted was highly irritating to Uncle Bill, but with the children to help, he gathered more golden weed, which was brought ashore. The centaurs wanted to eat it right away and came crowding around. Really, they were so big and strong that with the smallest show of force they could have readily got the golden weed and gone off without giving any information. But either this did not occur to them or (though Uncle Bill would not admit this) they had a strong sense of honor. For, seeing the golden weed, they left it alone, expressed themselves satisfied with the quantity, and started ruminating about what they'd seen in their journeyings around the land.

At first it seemed that they hadn't seen very much that was out of the ordinary. All other creatures they called "coves," and they spoke of a cove eating a prickly plant, and a cove with two other coves in a cave, and a crowd of coves climbing the other side of the mountain, and such incidents, which were really not out of the ordinary.

"Nothing more?" asked Uncle Bill, disappointed.

"Wot do you want, Shiny?" demanded Herman. "Egg in yer beer?"

"I was hoping you had seen something really remarkable," said Uncle Bill.

"What about the still cove?" said another.

" 'at's right," cried Herman. "Blimey, I'd forgotten about 'im. Gave me a real turn when I seen 'im. Over in Black Valley, on the other side of the land, there's a still cove. Lying down. 'asn't moved in four days. Maybe five. Real still."

"What kind of a cove?" asked Uncle Bill.

"Just a cove," said Herman. "Can't figure out why 'e don't move."

"He doesn't move because he's dead," said Uncle Bill.

"Dead?" cried the centaurs. "What kind of a thing is dead, Shiny?"

"Death is the gift of Ka, the Smiler," said Uncle Bill. "He brought it first to Earth. And now he has brought it to Nede." At this the centaurs for the first time ceased their prancing and jostling and stood as still as marble.

CHAPTER NINETEEN

UNCLE BILL was in a hurry to get to the Black Valley, where what the centaurs described as a "still cove" was lying. He did not, of course, know what kind of creature was meant but guessed that it must be dead if it had been lying without movement for four days or more. He therefore called the lumens to take him and the children across the island, and in a moment they were whisked up the slopes of the mountain and down the other side, and across a valley that was patterned like a chessboard in squares, but the squares were blue and black, and then over some hills that were a pleasant green, with silver streams flowing down them to the Seesuch, and then over a lovely scarlet plain with silver waves flowing over it when the wind blew.

Uncle Bill explained that the plain was covered with flamingo grass which was red on top and silver below, and the ruffling of the grass in the wind accounted for the silver waves. Beyond that, they came to a most curious forest, which looked like hundreds of acres of colored balloons attached to the ground by long strings.

"Balloon trees," said Uncle Bill. "The sap, which is lighter than air, flows up the thin stems and fills the balloon envelopes at the top. If you cut the stem, the balloons float off, higher and higher, until they finally explode from interior pressure."

"Does the sap taste good?" asked Kevin, happy to discover that although he was being whisked through the air at several hundred miles an hour, he was quite comfortable and could talk readily.

"Like lemonade, but with the texture of cream," said Uncle Bill. "In what corresponds to autumn on Nede, when the balloon trees ripen, hundreds of thousands of those balloons break off, float up in the air, and burst, and it rains a kind of creamy lemonade all over the place. Confounded nuisance."

"Gosh," said Kevin. "I should think it would be kind of nice to have creamy lemonade raining down on you."

"When you have a beard, it isn't nice at all," said Uncle Bill.

"Why does it come down if it is lighter than the air?" asked Christopher.

"There are traces of sodium sulfate in the sap, which in time attracts moisture from the air and so forms droplets that fall as rain," said Uncle Bill. "Now let us cut out the conversation, because I want to think. Try to figure out a few things for yourselves." But at that moment Patricia gave a horrified cry.

"Where's Arabella?" she said. The looked around, but Arabella was not to be seen, though Ita was with Una and Strike Three. The lumens didn't know what had happened to her. The last time anyone remembered seeing her was when she was straightening her hair with the aid of the mermaid's mirror. That was clue enough for Kevin.

"I bet she went into the Seesuch to find the mermaid and give her back her mirror," he said.

"If she's in the Seesuch, she can't come to any harm," said Uncle Bill. "Come on. We've got to get to the Black Valley. The whole future of Nede may be decided there for thousands of years to come."

"I'm going to look for Arabella," said Kevin. "I'm not going to leave her lost. She's probably looking all over the place for us. And probably frightened out of her wits."

"To judge by the way she spoke to those centaurs," said Uncle Bill, "I would think the opposite was the case. All right. You children go and look for Arabella. I must go on. And the lumens must come with me. I'm sure that Ka is in the Black Valley. The lumens have to meet and deal with him."

"Right now?" demanded Kevin. "Can't that wait until we find Arabella?"

"Right now," said Uncle Bill. "It can't wait. You don't know Ka. He's probably been around the Black Valley for some days. He's already brought death here.

His next gifts will be plague and famine and hate and war. Don't you understand that that's more important than finding Arabella?"

"You deal with Ka," said Kevin. "I'm going to look for Arabella. And at least let the lumens take us back to the Seesuch by the cliffs where the mermaids live."

"Oh, all right," said Uncle Bill. They were taken back to the tall cliffs by the Seesuch at whose foot the mermaids lived, and there, entering the Seesuch, they parted with Uncle Bill and the lumens, who sped off immediately to the Black Valley.

Worried as the children were about Arabella, as soon as they were below the surface of the Seesuch much of their anxiety left them, such was the effect of its soothing water on them. They swam down the jeweled face of the cliffs, only a little troubled about Arabella and actually beginning to enjoy themselves, and after a little while they found the mermaids.

They were sitting as before, their long dark hair undulating gently around their heads and shoulders and here and there a scale of their lower parts glittering like a diamond when caught by a ray of sunlight from above. They were singing a song about Jason, in what Kevin vaguely recognized as iambic pentameter, marking the syllables so nicely that all the children caught the rhythm and murmured in cadence,

"Tum tiddy tum tiddy tum
Tum tiddy tum tiddy tum."

When the song was done, Kevin said, "Mermaids. Please forgive us for interrupting you. We are looking for our little sister, Arabella. She found the mirror that one of you had lost, and we think she may have brought it back. Have you seen her, please?"

The mermaids looked very sadly at Kevin, and the principal one, who had stated that her name was written in the stars, took up her lyre and sang:

> *"The little one with the looking glass,*
> *Your sister who is gone,*
> *Went where mermaids may not pass,*
> *Far beyond high Matalin's mass.*
> *Went, and went alone."*

"Oh, gosh," said Kevin. "She gave them back the mirror and then set out to look for us and is climbing the mountain on foot."

Made nervous by this news, the children hardly stopped to say goodbye to the mermaids but swam to the surface and climbed the jeweled cliffs, which took them close to half an hour. When they got to the top, they found that despite their exertions they were not very tired, such was the effect of the air of Nede. They were standing on the glittering exercise track of the centaurs, and this gave Christopher an idea.

"Listen," he said. "Maybe if we got some golden weed we could get the centaurs to give us a ride, and they can search the whole place real quick for Arabella. That way we can find her and get back to Uncle Bill, in case he needs us. Uncle Bill said their sight is the keenest of any creatures in Nede, so they would soon find her."

"Yes, but where will we find the centaurs?" asked Kevin. "They've finished exercising by now and have gone to their own valley. And I don't know where that is."

"It must be somewhere over toward the mountain," said Patricia. "Oh, do let's get some golden weed and ask the centaurs to help. I really am scared for Arabella." And indeed she was, for she was nearly crying.

Rather than climb down the cliff again, they ran along the top until they came to the place where the cliff's edge plunged downhill to the shore. Here they waded into the Seesuch, dived down, and found lots of golden weed, which they carried up. And then, hustling as fast as they could, they set off toward the mountain of Matalin, looking for the valley of the centaurs.

It was fortunate that they had brought the golden weed. Otherwise, they might have had a hard time finding the valley the centaurs lived in, for there were many valleys, each a good distance apart and divided by ridges in the folds of the mountain's flank. But the centaurs, besides having keen sight, had a keen sense of smell, and they soon scented the weed and came thundering toward the children, who gave them the weed freely, at the same time begging them to help find Arabella.

"Wot? Little Tich?" said Herman. "Done a bunk, 'as she? Narsty, sneaky little thing, she is."

"Young 'uns are a proper caution these days," said another. "Turn yer back, and off they pop."

"Up to no good, that one," said Herman, munching away contentedly. "Could tell it when I clapped my eye on 'er. Proper little snake in the grass, if you ask me."

"She's nothing of the sort," said Patricia, and although she didn't mean to do it, she was so angry she slapped Herman on his velvet muzzle.

"Blimey," said Herman, starting back. "You gonna' spend the rest of yer natural popping me on the beak?"

"Making a kind of a career out of it, she is," said another. "Old 'erman opens his box and whap—right on the old horn."

"No warning," said a third. "Chopped 'im right on the chops with 'er mauley."

"Quick as silver," said a fourth. "Been practicing for years. No wonder little tich run off. Says 'good morning' and gets it right in the letterbox."

"I'm sorry," said Patricia. "Please, please, do believe me. I'm really sorry. But I'm worried about my little sister. We don't know where she is. She's lost and we think she may be hurt, and it's all so strange here . . ." And she broke into tears.

"Nah, then," said Herman. "Wot's all this? Crying? Can't 'ave that. 'ere. Cheer up, chum. Take another pop at me schnozzle if it'll make yer happy."

" 'at's right," said another. "Mustn't cry. Take a swing and stiffen me lip for me if it'll cheer yer 'eart." And so they went on, all offering their muzzles as a target if it would get Patricia to stop crying, and soon she had dried her tears and was smiling, because it was plain that all the centaurs were really very goodhearted creatures, though when they got hold of an idea or impression, they never let go of it.

"We were wondering if you would help us find Arabella," said Kevin.

"Easy as kiss me 'and," said Herman. "You want to stay 'ere while we trot around and 'ave a dekko?"

"Couldn't you take us with you?" Kevin asked.

Herman looked at Kevin with some compassion. "Wot do yer think yer are, mate?" he asked. "Blinking bolt of lightning on two legs? Yer can't keep up wiv us centaurs."

"We thought you might give us a ride on your backs," said Kevin quite humbly.

"Easy, mate," said Herman, greatly offended. "Come down off the chandelier. You didn't really think that we'd let yer get up on our backs, did you?"

"Blown 'is top," said another.

"Climbing straight up the bloomin' wall, 'e is."

"They gave 'im a nut bar and now 'e's nuts."

So they went on pooh-poohing the idea while Christopher—his head cocked on one side and his eyes screwed up—considered them. "That's all right," he said. "We didn't realize that you can't run fast if you have someone on your backs."

"Wot do yer mean, can't run fast. 'op up and find out," cried one.

"Come on," said another. "Up you get, and hold on tight."

"Put yer flippers under me wings, will yer," said Herman to Patricia, who had climbed on his back. "Don't want another swipe on the smeller when I'm least expecting it."

"Oh, I won't hit you again, Herman dear," said Patricia.

"Nah," said Herman with heavy sarcasm. "And it ain't gonna rain no more. Just put your dukes where you can't use 'em fast, and I'll be 'appy." So Patricia put her hands under Herman's wings—they were so dark a blue as to be almost black, and feathered with shining plumes which, on Patricia's inquiry, Herman said were horse feathers.

Then the centaurs took off, so fast that the landscape instantly lost all detail and became a blur, and the wind tore past the mounted children like a fresh gale, so that they had to close their eyes and hold on for dear life, leaving all the looking to the keen eyes of the centaurs.

In no time at all, the centaurs had explored the whole of the land, mountain valley, forest, and plain. When they went through the forest of balloon trees, they cut a path clean through the forest, leaving a trail of balloons floating up in the sky. But the path did not remain long. Immediately tiny balloons, no bigger than mushrooms, began forming on the ground, and soon the swath cut through the forest was filled again with balloon trees.

Not only was it impossible to see anything because of the gale winds that the centaurs raised in their galloping, but it was likewise impossible to hear, for the wind roared and shrieked past the children's ears, drowning out all other sounds.

Then Herman, Patricia's centaur, stopped so suddenly that if she had not been holding on to his wings she would have been thrown over his head a distance of at least a hundred yards. Immediately upon stopping, he gave a loud whistling neigh and all the other centaurs came thundering in from all points of the compass. Without even being told, Patricia knew that they were in the Black Valley, for all around, the ground glistened black as jet.

"Found tich," said Herman. "Just caught a glimpse of 'er out of the corner of me eye. 'iding, she is."

"Where?" cried Patricia.

"Right in that cave there," said Herman. "She's inside of a big green bowl. Tich and that still cove and the mirror. And Old Smiler is curled around it outside, 'issing with pleasure. Proper snake in the grass, 'e is. Well. Ta-ta."

And off the centaurs went in a whirlwind, leaving the children, who had dismounted, staring apprehensively at the entrance to the cave.

CHAPTER TWENTY

LED by Kevin, the children went cautiously into the cave, creeping along, their nerves alert for any danger. The light was gone as soon as they were a few feet inside, and they had to feel their way along the cold smooth walls, Kevin ahead and the others holding hands so as not to get separated.

After a few yards, a vague whisp of greenish light appeared ahead, and this increased in strength as they approached, until, rounding a bend in the corridor, they found before them a huge open area, drenched in a green light, the color of cheap lemonade.

In the middle of this area was a green bowl, of large size and shaped rather like the kind of bowl ladies keep face powder in on a dressing table. It had a lid on the top, and it was about the size of a house, though not as high. Curled around the bottom of this bowl lay Ka, the Smiler. The children did not recognize him immediately. He had arranged himself artfully so that his sinuous and gleaming body looked like some kind of decora-

Alice Wadowski-Bak

tion around the base of the bowl. His body was boldly enameled in red, black, and yellow, each color the shape of a diamond and therefore somewhat like scales. But the body of Ka was covered not by scales but by feathers. He appeared then as a feathered serpent, perhaps a hundred feet in length and with a head as big as a watermelon. The top portion of his head, including the flat skull, the eyes and nose, and down to the upper part of the mouth, was scarlet. The lower portion, that is to say, the thin lower jaw, was sulfur yellow. The division of these two colors on his face, coming at the mouth, gave Ka the appearance of smiling, and it was from this that he got his nickname, the Smiler.

At first, then, the children did not recognize him but were appalled at the size and cold beauty of the huge jade-green bowl in which Arabella was imprisoned. But then Ka moved and from a decoration became a serpent. He quickly unreeled several yards of himself from around the base of the bowl, arched upward and settled his head and several feet of his body on the lid of the bowl, and watched the children for a while out of amethyst eyes. Then he flicked a forked and thin purple tongue around his slit of a mouth, preparatory to speaking, or as if anticipating a meal.

This done, he said in a dreadful sibilant voice, "Dear little children. How sweet of you to come and find poor old lonely Ka. Such nice children. Do come a little nearer so I can see you better. My eyes are not of the best."

"Don't talk to him," bellowed Uncle Bill's voice. "And don't try to come and get us. Get away from here."

"Uncle Bill's inside too," said Christopher, and Patricia said very weakly, "Oh," and then said nothing more.

Ka slid a few more glittering yards of himself from the base of the bowl to the top. He raised up his head, five or six feet above his perch, and, moving it from side to side, addressed the children.

"Don't be afraid of poor old Ka," he lisped. "Ka will do anything you want. Anything at all. Anything. Anything. Yesss. Yessss. Just ask. You'll see." His voice was soft and almost intimate, and it was, then, all the more terrible for the children that so endearing and coaxing a voice should come from so monstrous a creature. Indeed, they were terrified by both the sight and the sound of Ka, and the smiling serpent started undulating from side to side, saying in a monotonous voice, "Come to Ka. Come to Ka. Come to Ka." He said this in rhythm with his sideways movements, and this combination of sound and sight in unison had a hypnotic effect on the children. They were frozen like rabbits before a rattlesnake, and had Ka struck at any one of them at that moment, or dropped a huge feathered loop around them all to trap them, they could have done nothing to defend themselves from him.

"Move," cried Uncle Bill from within the bowl, his voice heavily muffled. "Move. Do something. Don't stand still. Fight him."

"A little closer," lisped Ka. "A little closer, please," and he gyrated more rapidly, his purple tongue flicking over his smiling mouth in horrid anticipation. The very horror of the creature aroused a reaction in Kevin compounded of both fear and anger or perhaps shame. "Stay where you are," he said to the others. "Patricia! Wake up." It seemed to him that his sister had gone into a sort of doze on her feet, a doze in which her eyes remained open but her stare was quite vacant.

"A little closer," lisped Ka. "Just a tiny eensy bit clossser." He raised himself higher above the lid of his bowl until there were perhaps fifteen feet of his brightly colored scintillating body towering over the children. Christopher, more thoughtful than the others, had been the least affected by Ka, and now he squinted up his eyes and cocked his head on one side and whispered to Kevin, "I think I know something about Ka."

"What?" asked Kevin, and the very fact that he could talk to his brother relieved him of some of his fears.

"He's trying to trick us," said Christopher. "He really wants us to stay away or back up. That's why he keeps telling us to come a little closer. He knows that we're frightened and will do just the opposite."

"Why would he want us to back up?" asked Kevin, not taking his eyes off Ka for a moment.

"Because he can't see us when we are close," said Christopher. "See the way he moves his head from side to side and keeps going higher? He's trying to get us in focus. So long as we can stay a kind of blur, we're safe. What we should do is move in closer."

"Gosh," said Kevin. "That's what he keeps asking us to do. Supposing that's just what he wants?"

"You stay here," said Christopher. "I'll move in. When I've done that, you ask him how many of us there are." Christopher was pretty good at stealing bases, and he slid, quick as a mouse, from where he had been standing next to Kevin to the base of Ka's bowl, where he stopped.

Then Kevin said, "Ka. Ka the Smiler. Tell me how many of us there are here."

"Three," lisped Ka. "Three nice lovely adorable children." He was swinging quite rapidly but stopped and started counting and said, "One . . . Two . . ." Then he stopped. "What happened to the other one?" he asked. "What happened to the other pretty nice little strong boy?"

Kevin didn't answer. He seized Patricia by the hand and darted toward the base of the bowl to join Christopher. This threw Ka into a fury. He started whirling around the bowl, darting his huge melon head here and there, up and down, forward and backward, trying to get far enough away from the children to bring them into focus. All the time he hissed, "Where are my beautiful little children? Oh, where are they? Where have my pretty little children gone?"

"I wonder if there are lumens in the bowl too," said Patricia.

"No. We're here," answered Plutonius. "Only, we have no light, so Ka can't see us."

"What happened?" asked Christopher.

"Ka got the mermaid first," said Plutonius. "She was looking for her mirror and was told by Ka that he could take her to it. He carried her to the Black Valley and left her to make her change."

"Make her change?" said Patricia.

"He means to make her die," said Kevin.

"Yes," said Plutonius. "Mermaids must have their mirrors or they will die. That has never happened in Nede before. But it is what Ka wants, so he can start to rule here. The other mermaids told Arabella where to find her, and she came here through the Seesuch on a dolphin and so got here before Uncle Bill or the centaurs. The Seesuch is close to the Black Valley on this side of the land. But Ka then put the mermaid in his bowl and told Arabella she could save her if she got into the bowl with thc mirror. Which shc did."

"And then I suppose he told Uncle Bill he could save Arabella if he did the same?"

"Yes," said Plutonius. "But the Impatient Wise One knew that was not so. He suspected that once you are in Ka's bowl you cannot get out again. So he moved away to think about how to rescue Arabella, and Ka, as soon as he could see him clearly, seized him and put him in the bowl. And then you came."

Ka had by now stopped whirling and lashing about and had collapsed on top of his bowl, though a large portion of his body was still coiled around the base. He was hissing and twitching and whining to himself a little and saying, "Such pretty children for Ka. Such nice children for Ka. All lost. All lost." Kevin began to feel more disgusted at him than frightened. He said to Plutonius. "Is Ka deaf?"

"Yes," said Plutonius. "He can receive only heavy vibrations."

"And he's almost blind?"

"Less than the distance of his own length, he is blind," replied Plutonius. "Beyond that, his eyes are very sharp."

"We've got to get Arabella and Uncle Bill out of that bowl," said Kevin. "And the only way to do that is to entice Ka away from it."

To this, Plutonius said nothing.

"If you move beyond Ka's length and then light up he will see you and may go after you," said Kevin.

"But Ka cannot hold us. We have no bodies," said the lumens all together.

"It isn't our bodies he is after," said Plutonius. "It is ourselves. That is what Ka came here for. To master us lumens."

"How can he do that?" asked Kevin.

"I don't know," said Plutonius. "It is something to do with his bowl. Ka is very cunning. We can see what is going on in your mind. But we cannot see what is going on in Ka's mind. His vibrations, when we try, paralyze us."

"How did Uncle Bill say you lumens were to defeat Ka and drive him away from Nede?" asked Christopher.

"He didn't say," said Plutonius. "He didn't know himself. He thought we would find out when we met Ka. But we have found out nothing. And now we have lost the Impatient Wise One and Arabella."

"Why does he stay on top of his bowl?" asked Kevin.

"Because he loves his bowl," said Plutonius. "It is his special place where he can coil up with himself. He will never leave his bowl."

Kevin thought about this and said, "I'm going to talk to Ka. Everybody be quiet." Then he shouted, "Hey, Ka! Ka! Can you hear me? Answer me."

"Where are you? Oh, where are you, my beautiful boy?" hissed Ka. "Are you very close to Ka? Are you under the bowl of Ka?" cried the Smiler.

"Never mind where I am," said Kevin. "I want to help you. That's why I'm here." To this Ka made no reply. He stopped his slight hissing, becoming at once cautious and attentive.

"We heard you were in the cave in the Black Valley and had left your bowl outside, so that's why we came here, to see if you are sick."

"Left my bowl outside—left my lovely bowl?" cried Ka. "Oh, no. I'd never leave my bowl. I'm lying on it right now."

"That's it," said Kevin. "What you're lying on is a smooth black rock. It isn't your bowl at all. Your bowl is outside the cave, in the sun."

"Outside in the sun?" cried Ka, very agitated. "Outside the cave in the sun? Oh, no. It can't be. It mustn't be. It won't be. It never will be. The light will spoil my beautiful bowl. Oh, my beautiful bowl. But of course it isn't. I'm lying on my bowl. I can feel my bowl. So smooth and green. It's lovely."

"It's smooth all right," said Kevin. "But it's black. It's a rock. Your bowl is outside. It's getting a little crumbly in the sun."

This threw the serpent into a panic. It started to slide, whirling around its bowl, slipping from top to bottom and bottom to top, darting its tongue about to feel its surface, hissing enormously and making a tremendous rustling with its feathers. Eventually it settled down and said, "You lied to poor old lovable blind Ka. This is Ka's own bowl—his nice comforting bowl that he sleeps in and hides in and makes happiness in. His very, very own, lovely bowl."

The children, while Ka had been sliding and whirling around the bowl, had been hard put to stay out of his way, and darting here and there among his speeding coils, were a little out of breath themselves. But Kevin said, "All right. If you want to take a rock that is shaped like your bowl for a bowl, that's your business. We warned you. The real bowl is lying outside and getting crumbly in the sun."

"It's not," hissed Ka. "It's not. Ka's beautiful bowl is here."

"Crumbling away, minute by minute," said Kevin.

"You are lying to nice Ka," said the Smiler.

"All right," said Kevin. "See if I'm lying. You think that you're lying on the top of your bowl. Well, just try to take the top off."

"Oh, no," said Ka. "Oh, no. You want Ka to take the top off so his little guests can get out."

"You lumens ready?" whispered Kevin.

"We're afraid," said Plutonius. "If we are caught in the bowl when he puts the lid back on, we are lost forever."

"Well, so's Uncle Bill and Arabella and the mermaid, unless we get them out," said Kevin. "Look," he shouted to Ka. "Just lift the top up and put it right back down again. They can't move fast enough to get out."

"Ah, but you want them out, don't you?" hissed Ka.

"No," said Kevin, "because they are not in there. All you are lying on is a black rock."

Ka said nothing for a while but thrust here and there with his huge head, rearing it forward and backward to get a glimpse of the children, who crouched together on the far side of the bowl.

"How do you know about my bowl?" asked Ka eventually.

"The lumens told us," said Kevin.

"Lumens," hissed Ka. "Are there lumens here?"

"No. All outside. They don't like you."

"Bring them in," said Ka. "Oh, do bring them in. Bring them in and get them into my bowl, and the others can go free. Oh, please, please, be nice to poor old Ka and give him some lumens."

"All right," said Kevin. "But remember that your bowl is outside. You are coiled up on a smooth rock. You can prove that by trying to lift the top off that black rock you're lying on, that the lumens put there to trick you."

The thought of being tricked by the lumens threw Ka into a fury. He slipped, hissing, off the top of the bowl, reared up, seized the handle in its center in his mouth, and jerked the lid up. That was enough for the lumens. They darted to the bowl and quick as a flash had Uncle Bill, Arabella, and the mermaid and her mirror out. But a second later Plutonius cried in an agonized voice, "Ita! Little Ita! She got trapped inside. She is lost forever."

This news paralyzed the children, and it was more than Arabella was prepared to tolerate. She had had a thoroughly unhappy time in the bowl and had first cried and then started thinking and now she was mad. Although she wasn't very big, she could contain a great deal of wrath, and the thought of Ita, her personal lumen, being trapped in the green bowl brought her to boiling point. She looked about for a weapon, and finding only the mermaid's mirror, snatched it from her and started banging on Ka's feathered body, crying, "You let Ita out. You let her out, you old long feather duster, you."

Ka, surprised, reared up and darted his huge head down toward Arabella to seize her. But he was thrown back immediately with great force and lay hissing on the ground as if he had been struck a monstrous blow.

"The mirror," cried Christopher. "He can't stand to see himself in the mirror."

It was true. Unlike ordinary mirrors, that of the mermaid gave off its own light, enough for Ka to see his own features in. And the sight of his own countenance filled him with such agony that he lay writhing on the floor of the cave.

"Quick. Let's get Ita out," said Kevin, and he and Christopher and the lumens flew to the top of the bowl and wrenched it off, and out came the little lumen. Then, all working together, they took the lid of the bowl and threw it over the side so that it fell to the floor and splintered. And then, with the mermaid's mirror to repel Ka, they made their way out of the cave and to the safety of the Seesuch.

That night, when Venus rose above Nede like a malevolent red moon, they saw, peering up through the surface of the Seesuch, the feathered shape of Ka returning to his own planet with his broken bowl held in his coils. And they heard or seemed to hear him hissing, "Poor Ka. His lovely bowl is broken. Poor Ka. He has to mend his lovely bowl."

"He has been defeated and will not come back," said Plutonius.

"He will come back," said Uncle Bill. "But by then you will be stronger, and now that you know his nature, you will not be in such danger from him."

"I do not understand about his bowl," said Strike Three. "Why cannot we lumens get out of that bowl once we get into it? We can get out of anywhere else."

"You answer," said Uncle Bill to Plutonius.

Plutonius thought for a long while and said, "Ka is self-love. And his bowl is the bowl of self-love. And those who enter there get worse and worse and cannot get out of it until they help someone else."

And as he said this, his light did not diminish but instead grew a great deal brighter. And that pleased Uncle Bill even more than being rescued.

* · * · * · * · * · * · * · *

CHAPTER TWENTY-ONE

THE following day and for several days thereafter, the lumens, led by Plutonius, held a celebration of their victory over Ka and their evolvement (rapidly advancing) into individual rather than collective creatures. Uncle Bill explained that Ka could not have stopped this evolution, which was part of the Plan. But what he had intended to do was to turn it to his own ends. By bringing the lumens under his sway, he could have made them entirely self-centered, prepared to do nothing for anyone else, capable of no concern for the good of their fellows and of no cooperation that involved personal sacrifice or discomfort.

"That was the choice the lumens had to make," he said. "Between self and others. It was the choice put before man billions of years ago. At that time Cain, having killed his brother, replied for all humanity when he said, 'I am not my brother's keeper.' Ita, in her concern for Arabella, and the other lumens in their concern for us have shown that they are their brother's

keeper. So they will perhaps be able to avoid the wars and devastations and famines which we on Earth have endured through the centuries, until we learn, as I believe we are learning now, to reverse the terrible statement of Cain and be concerned for our brother."

To Uncle Bill's disgust, the children were treated as the heroes of the whole affair and were taken to the top of a beautiful golden mountain on the other side of the land from the Black Valley, where a review of the creatures of Nede was held in their honor. Whole swarms of lumens went past them like the passage of the Milky Way before their eyes, and these were followed by centaurs and gryphons and gorgons and all kinds of magnificent creatures, battalion by battalion, hour after hour.

The gryphons whirled splendidly about, their scarlet bodies magnificent against their blue enameled wings, and took the children for flights about the land. The wyverns, not to be outdone, begged the children to ride on their backs down into the dark caves of Nede, where they saw splendid treasure houses of emeralds, opals, diamonds, amethysts, and pearls, of all of which the wyverns were the guardians. They spoke with a lilting voice, like Welchmen.

Nobody, not even Plutonius, was allowed to accompany the children to see the treasure which the wyverns guarded and which was kept secret from all the other creatures on Nede. However, the wyverns offered Patricia a beautiful diamond pendant, as lovely as a drop of water, and Arabella a ruby as red as the seed of a ripe pomegranate. Such gifts the children could not resist, and the wyverns, who were small dragons and whose last home on earth had been Wales, were so pleased that they gathered together and roared a song for the children which they were sure must have made the whole mountain shake.

The title of the song, they gave very formally, as "Rhyfelgyrch Gwyr Harlech," which didn't mean anything to the children, but they recognized the tune as that of "Men of Harlech." When they had finished the last thundering chorus, the wyverns were silent and immobile for several seconds and then they fell on each other, wyvern embracing wyvern in a great flapping of enameled wings and clattering of scales, all saying how beautifully each had sung.

Then they took the children out of the cave, and when they got into the light, Patricia's beautiful diamond became a drop of water and Arabella's lovely ruby a pomegranate seed. The children were disappointed and Arabella a little mad, but then they smiled and the wyverns (who always spoke in a chorus, with altos, sopranos, tenors, and basses properly apportioned) said, "There is wisdom in that, look you. For a song is as good as a precious stone, and so we will sing for you again." And they did, announcing the title of the song as "Llwynon," which turned out to be "The Ash Grove." Then, wishing the children protection from all enemies (and especially the Saxons), the

wyverns returned to guarding their treasures . . . and singing.

These were but incidents in the triumphs of the land, which were matched in the Seesuch, where sea elephants and dolphins and sea horses, surgeon fish, fiddler crabs, snapping shrimps, pipe fish, and hosts of other creatures put on displays to honor the children.

Uncle Bill was a little touchy about the whole business, for he felt that after all he had had some part in the safeguarding of the lumens from the threat of Ka. It was a little galling then to have Kevin formally titled Kevin the Leader, and his brother, Christopher the Thinker, and Patricia become Patricia the Good, and Arabella become the Furious Warrior, while he got no new honors but retained his old title of the Impatient Wise One, which he could scarcely endure since it contained, in his belief, an unjust and libelous reflection on his character. However, a very special honor did await Uncle Bill, and this was bestowed on him in the Seesuch.

They were taken by Plutonius to the Jeweled Cliffs, and in the presence of regiments of sea horses and sea elephants and all the lovely creatures of the seas of Nede, the mermaids appeared before Uncle Bill (the first time he had ever seen them) and laid a wreath of sea anemones around his neck—which was the first time he had ever seen them, too.

Then the leader of the mermaids, taking up her lyre,

sang this little song to Uncle Bill, which was really a riddle:

> *"Wise one who travels through the stars,*
> *Who am I, who rival Mars?*
> *Great will be your Neden fame*
> *If you can divine my name.*
> *You then, master of the skies,*
> *Prove if you are truly wise."*

"And very nice indeed," said Uncle Bill. "You children will note that that little sextet starts and ends with the same word—wise. That is a little trick of the Arabian poetasters or rhymemakers, and that it should be used by this young lady indicates that the Arabian world had far more influence on the poetry of the golden period of Greece than our present-day scholars are prepared to allow.

"If you children had not been the victims of a modern education . . ."

But the mermaid interrupted, singing:

> *"Behold, I asked you for my name,*
> *And now a lecture you declaim.*
> *You fling learning at my head,*
> *Pray, in place of stones, give me bread."*

"Young woman," roared Uncle Bill, his beard bristling as it did when he was aroused, "I would remind you that I am considerably older than you (this horrid exaggeration brought shocked looks from the children), and I demand that you show the proper respect in the presence of your elders. As for your name, anybody with the slightest pretenses to an education (he glared at the children) would know immediately that it is Antares, the star in the constellation of Scorpio, which because of its reddish tinge is called the rival of Mars."

"Eureka," cried the mermaids, striking their lyres in unison. "He has it." And then, this being the greatest honor that could be offered to any creature in Nede, they circled around Uncle Bill, as they were wont to circle around the Greek heroes of three thousand and more years before, and composed on the spot an epic to his courage, wisdom, strength, and cunning which he found so fitting that at the conclusion he was not the slightest bit angry with them.

More was to come, however. Antares produced a crown of laurels—an ancient crown given to the greatest of the Greeks—and placed it on Uncle Bill's head and proclaimed that thereafter he was to be known through Nede and through all space as "Champion of the Helpless and Hero of Heroes."

"A little exaggerated, of course," said Uncle Bill later to Plutonius and Kevin. "But one must make allowances for the enthusiasms of the Greeks."

The time came at last when they had to return to Earth, and though all the creatures of Nede tried to look happy, they were really very sad at the parting.

"Promise, Impatient Wise One," said Plutonius, "that the children will return to Nede."

"Oh, I expect they will," said Uncle Bill, who was feeling sad himself and, since he didn't like to show it, affected impatience. "They weren't such a confounded nuisance as I thought they were going to be. In fact, they were quite helpful." (Already the children's part in the rescue of the lumens was beginning to dim in his mind, and his own to grow.)

"Promise solemnly that they will come back," persisted Plutonius, and Strike Three, Una, and Ita began shouting, "Promise. Promise. We won't take you to Earth unless you promise."

"I'll promise," said Uncle Bill, "but it's up to them. If they want to get back here at all, they had better say nothing whatever to their father and mother about where they've been. They won't be believed, and it will be assumed that while they were at Coppertown with me I turned them into infernal liars."

"Gosh, I don't know how we can do that," said Christopher.

"It will be easy," said Patricia. "Leave everything to me."

And indeed it did turn out easy. For when the children's father met them at the airport in Los Angeles and drove them home and everybody had hugged everybody and they'd all settled down in their house, he turned to his wife and said, "I don't understand children these days. I asked those kids what happened at Coppertown, and Patricia said, 'Nothing.' And do you know what they're doing now? They're watching television. Just as if they'd never been anywhere."

"Children are so adaptable," said his wife. "Colorado or California, it doesn't make much difference to them. That's the comforting thing about them. It helps them get through a very puzzling world. What program are they watching by the way?"

" 'Lost in Space' or some other nonsense about flying saucers," said their father, and reaching for his evening paper, was himself soon lost in the sports pages.